✔ KU-251-997

Aberdeenshire Library and Information Service
www.aberdeenshire.gov.uk/libraries
Renewals Hotline 01224 661511

1 9 JUL 2011   1 1 JAN 2017

2 2 AUG 2011

2 0 FEB 2017

1 8 OCT 2013
− 3 MAR 2018

H Q
1 9 DEC 2014   2 4 SEP 2018

− 6 FEB 2015

2 8 APR 2015

1 6 SEP 201   1 0 JUN 2021

3 0 SEP 2015
1 6 FEB 2016
− 5 DEC 2016

2 8 DEC 2016

− 2 JAN 2017

ABERDEENSHIRE
LIBRARIES

WITHDRAWN
FROM LIBRARY

A L I S
1813605

SPY PUPS:
PRISON BREAK

Andrew Cope

First published in 2010
by Puffin Books,
a division of Penguin Books Ltd
This Large Print edition published by
AudioGO Ltd 2011
by arrangement with
Penguin Books Ltd

ISBN: 978 1405 664769

Text copyright © Andrew Cope, 2010

The moral right of the author
has been asserted

All rights reserved

British Library Cataloguing in Publication Data available

JLP

Printed and bound in Great Britain by
MPG Books Group Limited

For Aunty Kid and Uncle Martin

CONTENTS

1

TWENTY-FOUR HOURS

Today . . .

'I'm not sure I want to,' whined Star, her puppy eyes filled with worry. 'It's such a long way down.'

Spud frowned at her. His sister could be so annoying at times. *Here we are, about to do our first parachute jump, and my sis wants to back out!* 'Mum's life depends on us,' he barked gravely. 'She has less than twenty-four hours to live. We are her only chance of survival.'

Star nodded. *He's right*, she thought. *We are spy pups and this time we've got the most important mission of our lives.* She took a deep breath and stepped forward for Professor Cortex to fasten her helmet strap. *Please do it up tightly!*

'Are you spy pups ready?' bellowed the professor above the roar of the engines. Before the puppies were born the professor had trained their mum to be a spy dog and they knew he was desperate to save her.

Spud wagged hard. 'As I'll ever be,' he nodded.

All eyes fell on Star. She nodded bravely but her body language told another story. She was terrified of heights. She was sure she could tackle just about anything else—sharks, lions, evil villains, enemy spies—but falling from a plane was her ultimate fear. Star and Spud had had a recent adventure that involved sliding down a zip wire and that had made her worse.

'You OK, Agent Star?' asked Professor Cortex. 'You don't have to go through with it.'

Oh yes I do, Prof, she nodded. *This is a life-or-death situation.* Star took a deep breath and saluted the professor. 'Let's do it!'

Professor Cortex reached for the aeroplane door and hauled it open. A gale howled around the cabin, blowing his papers all over the place. 'It's now or never!' he yelled into the wind. 'There's your target.'

Spud bounded to the open door and

leant out into the dark night. Lights twinkled through the wispy clouds below. The puppy followed the professor's finger to a square patch of lights.

Spud breathed the fresh air. 'This is sooooo exciting!' he howled. 'Come on, sis, let's go for it.'

Star edged forward. 'I'm not so sure,' she said. 'It's a long way and it's dark.'

Spud snorted in frustration. 'This is a mission,' he barked. 'And we're in it together.'

He grabbed his sister's collar and hauled her out of the plane. Star disappeared into the night sky with a terrified yowl. Spud saluted the professor. *Best go and catch her up*, he wagged. 'Geronimooooo!' howled the spy puppy as he threw himself into the blackness outside.

The mission had started.

2

THAT DOG!

Three days ago . . .

Mr Big hated queuing. And in prison he had to queue for everything.

It's a good job it's only temporary, he thought as he offered his bowl to the man behind the counter.

His fellow inmate shouldn't really have been on serving duty. He had a streaming cold and Mr Big winced as he did a massive sneeze, sending a snot bomb into the saucepan. He blew his nose into his apron and continued serving. Some green slop was ladled into Mr Big's bowl.

'What's that supposed to be?' he grunted.

'Er, soup of the day,' replied the server, wiping his nose on the back of his hand.

'Which day?' asked Mr Big. 'It looks like something the dog's sicked up.'

'Probably is,' chuckled the man, filling the next inmate's bowl.

Mr Big knew there was no point in arguing. This wasn't any old prison. This was the world's most secure prison. It housed all the worst criminals on the planet and he was proud to be part of it. 'Normal criminals go to wishy-washy prisons,' he told his fellow inmates. 'It's an honour to be in this one. It means we're the real deal.'

Mr Big took a piece of stale bread from the basket at the end of the line and made his way to his usual table. 'Archie, Gus,' he nodded, 'how's the *soup de jour*?'

'Soup de what?' grunted Gus.

'It's French, stupid,' piped up Archie. 'The soup of the day is fantastic,' he smiled. 'And we won't be having too much more of it, will we, boss?' he beamed. 'Not if our plan comes off.'

'"When" not "if",' corrected Mr Big, picking up his spoon and grimacing. The server's sneeze globule was floating in the green goo. He was used to the finer things in life. His criminal mind had brought him wealth beyond the

imaginations of most people. He'd owned homes all over the world. He'd driven expensive cars and eaten in the world's finest restaurants. And now he was reduced to queuing for snot soup. All because of a dog. *That* dog! But his plan was kicking into action and soon that dratted spy dog would be in big trouble. If his information was correct, she'd had puppies and settled into the good life. Mr Big wasn't interested in the dog having a good life. Having *no life* was uppermost in his mind.

'Are we clear about the next step?' he asked, pushing his untouched soup to one side.

'Yes, boss,' replied Gus, finishing his own soup and reaching for Mr Big's. He lowered his head to bowl level and took a big spoonful. 'Yum,' he smiled, 'yours has got chewy bits.'

'Never mind the chewy bits, Gus,' sighed Mr Big. 'Do you understand the next step of the plan?'

'Our mole says the mutt's birthday is tomorrow,' he slurped. 'The gift should already be waiting. I hope she likes it. I wrapped it myself. It looks good.'

'Yes,' purred the evil criminal. 'Unlike the food in this joint, it's good enough to eat!'

3

BIRTHDAY TREAT

Two days ago . . .

The puppies were more excited than their mum. 'How old are you, Ma?' asked Star, bouncing with excitement. She had the same black and white splodges as her mother and was full of energy.

'Twenty-one,' she reminded her daughter. 'Again!'

'Is that dog years or human years?' yapped Spud, who looked more like his father, a handsome black pedigree called Potter.

'You work it out,' woofed Lara. 'And it's rude to ask a lady how old she is!'

Star jumped on to Sophie's knee for a cuddle but the excitement was too much and she couldn't settle.

The lounge door swung open and in walked Mrs Cook with a beam as big as the cake she was holding. The birthday candles flickered away.

Spud sniffed the air and started to salivate. 'I love cake,' he howled. 'Can I have an extra-large slice? Pleeease?'

Mr Cook conducted a chorus of 'Happy Birthday' for the family pet, the puppies joining in with hearty yapping. Star played along on the piano. It was difficult with paws instead of hands but she was improving fast.

Mrs Cook put the bone-shaped cake on to the coffee table and Lara beckoned to her puppies. 'Come on then, you two,' she woofed. 'Help me blow out the candles and then we can open some pressies.'

Ben, the eldest of the Cook children, photographed the dogs as they took deep breaths and blew out the candles in one go. Everyone cheered and Mrs Cook cut slices for everyone. Spud wolfed his down and came back for more, his tail almost wagging him off his feet.

Lara raised an eyebrow as she passed a small second helping to him. *His waistline isn't quite in keeping with a spy dog*, she thought. *But I'm sure it's just puppy fat.*

11

'Are you going to open your presents now, Lara?' asked Ollie, the youngest child. 'You've got loads. Especially for a dog.'

Lara eyed the pile of gift-wrapped presents and smiled a doggie smile. Most were in the shape of balls or bones so it was easy to guess what they were.

She let the puppies take turns in

12

ripping open the paper. 'Oh, a ball,' woofed Lara, planting a lick on Ollie's face. 'How very kind.'

'And another ball,' wagged Star, as her mum planted a lick on Sophie.

'A hat-trick of balls,' woofed Spud, nosing open another parcel. 'Good job they're your favourite thing, Ma.'

Lara wagged happily. *Not quite my favourite thing*, she thought, sniffing a beautifully wrapped package. Lara couldn't help wagging. *I know that smell! This is my favourite thing.* She checked the label. 'From your BIGGEST admirer,' she read. *It's nice to know I've got some admirers.*

Lara slid a claw down the side of the package and her eyes lit up. *My nose wasn't tricking me!* She looked at the pack of custard creams. *My absolute favourite!* she drooled. 'Not for sharing,' she woofed, wagging her paw at the puppies. 'Especially not you,' she glared at Spud. 'You lot can have the cake. These are Mum's *special* biscuits!'

Sophie grabbed one of Lara's new balls and headed for the garden. 'Anyone for a chase?' she sang as the three dogs bounded after her.

Mrs Cook tidied up all the wrapping paper. She looked at the custard creams and smiled. 'How thoughtful,' she said to herself as she put Mr Big's poisoned biscuits on the mantelpiece. 'Maybe she can have them as a treat later.'

4

A DOG'S DINNER

Lara soon gave up chasing the new balls. *One's OK*, she panted. *But three are exhausting!* She lay next to Sophie with her tongue hanging out of the side of her mouth. *Phew*, she panted, *I'm struggling to keep up with the pups.* She watched as Ben did one of his longest throws. Star beat her brother to the ball and then they chased each other around the garden to see who could bring it back to Ben, dropping it at his feet before waiting expectantly for the next throw.

I used to be fit, thought Lara. *Not that long ago, before I became a mum.* She recalled her spy-dog days. *All those cross-country fitness runs*, she remembered. *And army assault courses! I used to be able to do five hundred press-ups; now I'd be pushed to do five!*

In fact, Lara wasn't really her name at all. Licensed Assault and Rescue Animal, code name GM451, was proud to be the first graduate from Professor Cortex's animal spy school. 'Top of the class,' she panted. 'By a mile!' Lara put her paw to her bullet-holed ear and shuddered as she thought about some of the missions she'd been on. *Danger was my middle name*, she thought. *I've captured all sorts of baddies!*

Star dropped a frisbee at Lara's feet. 'Throw it, Mum,' she wagged. 'And I'll catch.'

Lara took the frisbee in her mouth and stood on her hind legs. With an expert flick of her head she launched the disc and watched as both her puppies scampered across the lawn in hot pursuit. Star was as lean and fit as Lara had been in her heyday. She leapt high above her brother and snatched the frisbee in her jaws, giving him the runaround before dropping it at her mum's feet.

'Again!' she panted.

The pups are a bundle of energy, thought Lara as her second throw got caught in a tree. Spud was on the case. He'd attached a rope to the trampoline for just such an emergency. He wasn't as

16

quick-thinking as his sister but he was an adventurous puppy. *And he shares my liking for bullet-holed ears*, thought Lara, remembering the puppies' first mission a few weeks ago.

Spud and Star worked together to haul the trampoline underneath the tree. Sophie applauded as the puppies bounced as high as they could until Star nosed the frisbee, Spud caught it and the chase started all over again.

'What a team,' laughed Sophie, proud that her pets were special.

Lara had officially retired from the Secret Service to concentrate on being a family pet. *Spying was a career. But now I'm a mum*, she thought, *adventure is off the menu! No more missions. No more baddies. Just having fun with my puppies and the kids.*

Lara loved her adopted family. She cast her mind back to her days in the RSPCA kennel. *I chose well*, she considered. *There were so many owners I could have gone home with, but these are the best. I knew it the minute I set eyes on the children.* Ollie was the youngest and the first to spot Lara's special skills. He'd heard her whistling at the dog kennels but nobody had believed him. Catching his pet sitting on the toilet reading the newspaper had put things beyond doubt.

'There's no way this is normal doggie behaviour,' he'd explained to his brother and sister. Ollie was also the chattiest of the children so even if Lara could speak she wouldn't have got a word in edgeways.

Sophie was very loving and caring. Lara loved it when the little girl brushed her fur so it shone. The puppies also adored Sophie. They'd often curl up on her knee for an evening snooze. Sophie was a very bright ten-year-old and helped the pups with their accelerated learning programme. Their current topics were capital cities and Victorian history.

As the oldest child, Ben was the leader. He loved having an ex-spy dog as a pet. Lara didn't like to boast but she knew she was extraordinary.

How many other dogs can defuse a bomb, pitch a tent and beat their owners on computer games? she thought. *But it's the simple things that I love.* Lara and Ben would often spend time out on their bikes or lazing by the river. Ben had been there when his pet had caught her first trout, the picture proudly framed by Lara's dog basket. *Yes,* she thought, *family life is total bliss.*

Lara trotted indoors to read her book. *It's not often I get any peace and quiet,* she thought as she settled into her favourite armchair. She secured her spectacles on the end of her nose and opened her Harry Potter book at the folded-over page to begin reading.

Lara fidgeted, scratched behind her ear and began reading again. And again. She couldn't get past the first paragraph. The special custard creams were in her line of vision. *I shouldn't,* she thought, ignoring her craving. But the paragraph wasn't sinking in. *It is my birthday. And they are my absolute fave. And I can perhaps go for a run afterwards?* she pondered.

Lara put her book down and trotted over to the mantelpiece. She sniffed the packet and closed her eyes with pleasure. *One won't hurt. And I only*

had a small slice of cake, she thought as she clawed open the packet. Her doggie nose sniffed again. *Oh boy*, she drooled, licking her chops. *They smell so gooood.*

Lara gobbled a biscuit. *Oh yes*, she thought, *they taste as good as they look.* Another followed. And another. Lara crunched her way through half the packet and then stopped to think. She brushed the crumbs off her book. *Half gone now*, she considered. *I should probably destroy the evidence.* With some furious chomping and a flurry of crumbs Lara polished off the rest of the poisoned biscuits before returning to her book.

5

A BIG PLAN

It looked as though Gus would fall through the top bunk. His huge frame hung down, restricting Archie's space in the bed below. The cell door opened and Mr Big strode in. Archie poked a bony finger into the saggy shape above. 'Boss is here, big man,' he shouted, and Gus sat up, dangling his legs over the side of the creaky bed.

'Is it time?' he asked.

My Big opened the cupboard and pulled out a laptop and a box of expensive cigars. He lit one and puffed out a cloud of grey smoke.

Archie started dancing about with excitement. 'I don't know how you do it, boss, but you always come up trumps. You've managed to smuggle a laptop into prison. Quick, let's get the recording done.'

Mr Big lifted the lid and took the script from his pocket as he waited for

the laptop to boot up. The end of his cigar glowed brightly as he sucked in another lungful of smoke. He looked at the box on the table. *Smoking is bad for your health* read the warning. 'And if you're a dog, so am I,' he chuckled to himself. Mr Big inserted a memory stick into the laptop and nodded to the others. 'Check the corridor,' he said. 'Here goes.'

Archie and Gus stood by the cell door while Mr Big got to work.

'Hello, doggie,' they heard him say. Gus cringed as Mr Big began to sing a tone-deaf version of 'Happy Birthday'.

'Many happy returns,' he soothed. 'I hope you had a lovely day. And I hope you know who this is?' His cigar glowed again. 'You want a clue? I am your BIGGEST admirer.' Mr Big disappeared into a fit of laughter, cut short by his smoker's cough. He cleared his throat. 'Anyway, poochie, I hope you enjoyed my pressie? Yummy biscuits. Your favourite, I believe? Me and the boys enjoyed making them. The biscuits are special, you see. They may smell like biscuits and look like biscuits. They even taste like biscuits. Do you know why?' Mr Big drew on his cigar before continuing. 'Because they *are* biscuits!' All of a sudden Mr Big's tone changed. He left a dramatic pause. '*Poisoned* biscuits,' he added in a cigar growl. 'We call them Killer Custard Creams.'

The evil criminal blew a smoke ring at the laptop. 'Here's the deal, poochie. You have three days—that's seventy-two hours—before the poison takes over completely. In that time you will break me and my boys out of this prison. I have the antidote. I am the only one who can save you. If we're not out in that time you will suffer a horrible, painful, glorious death and the world will be rid of Spy Dog. So,' he rumbled in his most gravelly voice, 'break me out and live. Or fail and die.'

Archie started jumping about. 'Guard coming, boss,' he hissed nervously, pointing out of the cell. 'Coming right this way.'

Mr Big stayed calm and finished his recording. 'I look forward to seeing you very soon,' he said, before adding a sentence he'd always dreamt of saying. 'Oh, and by the way, this message will self-destruct in fifteen seconds.'

'Quick, boss,' worried Archie, his hands waving in the air.

'Archie, calm down,' barked Mr Big. 'Gus, take care of it.'

The huge convict lumbered out of his cell and deliberately bumped into the prison guard, knocking him off his feet.

'Sorry, sir,' lied Gus, his gold teeth

glinting. He reached a hand down to help up the warden.

'You will be, idiot,' snapped the guard, getting to his feet and smoothing his uniform. 'Out of my way,' he glared, 'I want to check your cell. Someone's stolen a laptop from the office.'

Gus stood tall, his barrel chest blocking the entrance.

'I said, out of my way!' repeated the guard, reaching for his truncheon.

'It's OK, Gus,' shouted Mr Big. 'Let him past. We've nothing to hide. In fact, we've got something to show him.'

Gus stood aside and the officer pushed past and into the cell. His nostrils flared at the smell of tobacco. 'This is a no-smoking prison, Big,' he reminded. 'I hope you're not being a bad boy?' The guard shuffled nervously. Even the prison officers were afraid of Mr Big.

'A bad boy?' repeated the criminal, forcing a smile. 'Me? Far from it, sir. We found this,' he said, holding out the laptop. 'And we'd like to do the right thing and hand it in.'

'But—' began Gus, before being cut short by his boss.

'No buts, Gus,' soothed Mr Big. 'We're in prison because we've been naughty. Now we're learning to be good boys,' he growled. 'And then they'll let us out. Isn't that right, sir?'

'You'll never be let out,' said the warden bravely. He snatched the laptop and turned to leave when he had a thought. Mr Big was the most evil prisoner in the world's most evil prison. Why would he be giving the laptop back? He turned round. 'You'd better not be up to something, Big,' he warned. 'Nobody's ever escaped from here.'

The cell door slammed and the guard hurried away with the laptop.

Mr Big took the memory stick from inside his sock. 'Well, we like a challenge,' he grinned. 'Nobody's ever escaped because nobody's ever had a spy dog working on the outside,' he smirked. 'This goes in the post this afternoon and we'll be free by the weekend.'

6

THE RACE

It was the morning after Lara's birthday. Mr and Mrs Cook went to work and the children to school. Lara wasn't feeling well so she asked the puppies to run the morning pet neighbourhood-watch meeting. 'I'll have a bit of a lie-down,' she told them.

Lara had the house to herself. She nosed through the post and was

surprised to see a letter with her name on the front. *Unusual*, she thought. Lara chewed open the envelope and a computer memory stick dropped out. She rummaged in the package and fished out a piece of paper. *Play me*, it read.

Lara shrugged. She felt strangely weary. *I can't be bothered to turn on the computer*, she thought. *I'll play this later.*

Then she curled up on the sofa and fell into a deep sleep.

*　　　*　　　*

The puppies were having a fabulous time. The animal neighbourhood-watch

team gathered expectantly. They were in awe of Lara so her offspring were held in equally high regard.

'Our mum's feeling a bit under the weather,' woofed Star, 'so she's asked us to step in and run this session.'

Spud did the feline sign language to translate for the cats. They nodded approvingly.

'So what are we doing today?' asked Mindy, bouncing excitedly.

'Racing!' barked Star, watching her brother running on the spot for feline translation.

The cats hung their heads. They hated anything competitive.

George the tortoise disappeared into his shell. Racing wasn't his idea of fun either.

'We've decided to test out some new gadgets kindly donated by Professor Cortex. Dogs versus cats, versus George. We're going to see who can get into town and back the quickest.'

George's legs came out and he turned to go home. 'No point staying,' he murmured to himself. 'Town and back! That's a two-year trek for me!'

'Hey, George,' woofed Spud, 'don't give up so quickly. We have a surprise for you.'

George hesitated. He decided to give the puppies a chance.

'Who's the fastest dog?' woofed Star. 'Quickest in the neighbourhood? After me, of course.'

Danny Boy raised a paw. 'My mum was a greyhound,' he said proudly. 'So I'm pretty swift.'

'And puss cats?' woofed Star, her brother explaining in sign language once more. 'We need a volunteer to try these,' she said, holding up a pair of specially designed Rollerblades. 'And we've only got one cat crazy enough to try this,' she yapped, as her brother put his paw to his head to demonstrate.

Connie stepped forward importantly. She'd already used several of her nine lives, including the loss of half an ear in a cycling accident. 'They look fabulous,' she purred, lying down while Spud slipped the wheeled boots on to her tiny feet. Connie stood gingerly. 'Easy peasy,' she mewed, wobbling across the grass. She reached the concrete path and her

31

legs went in four different directions, sending her to the ground in a furry starfish shape.

The other cats gathered round and helped her up. There was no way they were going to lose to a dog!

'And you, George,' woofed Star, 'have had your skateboard upgraded!' Star produced a skateboard with a harness. George's neck stretched in excitement. 'It's . . . got . . . a . . .'

'Rocket on the back,' said Star, finishing his sentence. 'Which makes you the fastest tortoise in the world!'

'Probably the universe,' added Spud as the animals crowded round to examine

the professor's invention. 'Nought to sixty in three point seven seconds,' explained the spy pup. 'Controlled by George's head movements. This will transform tortoises the world over. And George is the guinea pig.'

Bullet the guinea pig raised his paw in objection as George was strapped into the harness. Spud clipped a small helmet to the reptile's bony head. 'Just in case, old fella,' he woofed.

'This is sooo exciting,' barked Danny Boy. 'Greyhound versus Rollerblading puss versus rocket-propelled tortoise! What are the rules?'

'No rules, guys,' yapped Spud. 'First to the marketplace and back is the winner. Simple as that. We've got Polly up there watching.' Everyone looked up at the parrot flying overhead. 'She'll be providing the commentary. And here's something else from the professor,' he woofed. 'GPS watches for all the competitors, so you don't get lost if . . . erm . . . you suddenly take a new direction,' he added, eyeing George's skateboard.

There was a murmur of excitement in the assembled crowd. This was a much more exciting meeting than Lara usually ran!

'Are you guys ready?' woofed Spud, switching on George's rocket and standing well back.

The animals nodded. 'Then off you go!' barked Star, waving a handkerchief to signal 'go'.

Danny Boy was away first. No gadgets or gimmicks—he was pure four-legged canine speed! Connie wobbled to the gate, hanging on to the fence like a beginner ice-skater. She let go and accelerated down the road, screeching in terror as she went.

George stalled his engine so had to be restarted. He chugged a little and some smoke blew out of the back. He worked the lever with his head and off he went, cautiously at first and then more confidently as he got on to the straight bit of road.

The race was on!

*   *   *

Lara was woken by a noise outside. *I feel awful*, she thought as she dragged herself over to the window. She watched as George spluttered by in a cloud of smoke.

That definitely looks like the work of the prof. She knew the pups shouldn't really be encouraging the pets to use gadgets in public. Normally Lara would have bounded outside and put a stop to the race.

I'll tell them off later, she thought. *I feel deathly. I think it was a mistake to eat so much cake and a whole packet of biscuits yesterday. But right now I'd better get to the bathroom. And quick!*

7

AN EVIL MESSAGE

Outside, the race was well and truly underway. Grandma Cook was walking up the cul-de-sac as Danny raced by.

'Hello, Danny Boy,' waved the old lady. 'And goodbye again,' she said as her favourite dog blurred past. Then from round the corner came a Rollerblading cat. 'Connie,' she said, dropping her shopping bag, 'is that you?'

'Meeeoooeow,' wailed Connie, unable to stop.

'You do see some amazing things nowadays,' muttered Gran, picking up her basket and setting off again. The old lady hadn't gone three steps before George hurtled round the corner. He'd taken it too fast and was clipping the hedge as he went.

'George?' said Gran, dropping her shopping again. The old lady leapt out of the way as the rocket-propelled reptile whizzed past in a cloud of smoke.

'Danny Boy is at the marketplace,' screeched Polly from above. 'George has just nudged into second place. Connie's crashed into a wall but looks OK.'

The dogs cheered. The cats hissed and sharpened their claws.

Danny was slowing. He might be half greyhound but his other half was Rottweiler—slow and ponderous. His muscles ached. He could hear George's engine spluttering behind.

Connie righted herself. She'd lost half of her other ear but it wasn't going to stop her. She desperately wanted to be the fastest pet. Lara would be so proud. The Rollerblading cat was growing in confidence and she was definitely gaining on Danny Boy. The pavement whizzed by as she caught up with the dog.

'Toodle pip, old fella,' waved Connie, looking back and smiling at the exhausted dog. 'Power to the felines—'

Slam!

Connie hit a tree—another of her lives gone—and Danny nudged back into second place.

George's engine was overheating. He could see the finish line but his shell was getting hot. The engine started to cough. Fifty metres to go. It felt like his shell was melting. Forty metres. The engine stalled and he was freewheeling the rest of the way. His skateboard wheels trundled across the tarmac but he was slowing. The tortoise swung his legs in a breaststroke motion to maintain momentum. He could hear Danny Boy's panting. He looked up to see the animals cheering. The dogs were wild, the cats wilder. George glided to a halt just before the line and the Rollerblading cat whizzed by, winning the race by a whisker.

There were joyous celebrations from the feline community and Connie was held up like the FA Cup. Danny Boy was a proud second. 'No gadgets,' he panted. 'Just sheer dog power.'

Polly flew down and nudged George over the line. Everyone agreed it was an excellent time for a tortoise.

'A tad more fuel, George, and the championship could have been yours!' she squawked.

Star and Spud brought drinks into the garden and the team slurped for a

while before disappearing back to their respective homes. Connie took her skates, the cats plotting some extra practice.

The puppies scampered indoors, proud at having chaired their first ever meeting of the pet neighbourhood-watch team. Their mum was fast asleep so they busied themselves in the kitchen.

Spud made himself a jam, ham and salami triple-decker sandwich while Star emptied the dishwasher. 'Hey, check this out,' she said, shutting the cutlery drawer. 'A memory stick and a note saying *Play me*.'

'Let's see what's on it,' barked Spud, spitting bread as he spoke.

The puppies galloped upstairs and slotted the stick into the family computer. Spud was the expert at holding a pencil in his mouth and he clicked a few keys to open up the correct software. 'It's an audio file,' he said. 'Let's see what it says.' He clicked the Play button and swivelled in his chair.

'Lovely but a bit out of tune,' woofed Star, listening to 'Happy Birthday'.

'Mum's got an admirer,' giggled Star.

Spud stopped swivelling and Star's wag died as Mr Big's message boomed from the speakers. Their mouths fell open as the evil laugh turned into a choking cough. 'So, break me out and live,' they heard him say, 'or fail and die.'

Spud's teeth were chattering as Mr Big finished his short message. 'Oh, and by the way, this message will self-destruct in fifteen seconds.'

Star was frozen with fear. 'Mum,' she whimpered. 'This evil man has poisoned her.'

Spud sprang into action. 'Fifteen seconds, sis!' he woofed 'What did he mean "self-destruct"?'

'What if Mum dies?' whined his sister, shocked at the message.

'If this self-destructs, we might die too!' woofed her brother, counting down in his head. 'Twelve, eleven, ten . . .'

Spud took the memory stick in his mouth and looked around frantically. He sprinted for the stairs. 'Eight, seven, six . . .' He half ran and half fell to the bottom, sped through the kitchen and outside to the wheelie bin.

'Three, two, one—'

He flipped the lid and tossed the memory stick inside. The lid banged shut and a small explosion raised it again, potato peelings and last night's curry spewing out.

Mmm curry!

Then smoke.

Then nothing.

8

A PUPPY PLAN

The Cook children gathered in Professor Cortex's lab. Ollie yawned loudly. It was very late but this was an emergency.

Lara lay with her head on her paws while Ben explained the story to the professor. 'It's Mr Big,' he said. 'Lara's arch-enemy. She's already captured him twice and it seems he's intent on revenge. He sent her some poisoned biscuits.'

'Which she scoffed in one go,' added Ollie a little too enthusiastically.

Lara hung her head, partly in shame and partly because she didn't have the energy to do anything else.

'And he's sent us a recording from prison saying she has seventy-two hours to live unless we break him out,' said Ben.

'Of the world's most maximum security prison!' added Sophie.

All eyes fell on the retired spy dog,

her sad eyes half shut. She was obviously unwell but the professor couldn't help asking. 'How are you feeling, GM451?'

The professor still found it hard to call Lara anything other than her code name.

How do you think? thought Lara, working hard to find the energy to lift a surprised eyebrow. *I didn't just nibble one poisoned biscuit, I wolfed the whole lot. Poorly tum. Headache. Dry nose. Plus I ate them yesterday, which means twenty-four hours have already gone.*

'You look absolutely dreadful,' agreed the professor, running a hand over his prized spy dog. The professor couldn't help noticing that her fur was falling out. 'Not good, GM451. In fact, verging on very bad indeed.'

Thanks, Prof, thought Lara, her eyebrows lowered and eyes closing with exhaustion.

'So what do we do, Professor?' asked Ben. 'Call the police and tell them everything?'

'That's doomed to failure,' nodded the professor over the top of his spectacles. 'The police would never agree to releasing the most dangerous prisoner they have.'

'It's a maximum security prison,' reminded Sophie. 'So we can't just break in. That'd really be too dangerous and silly, wouldn't it, Professor?'

'Er,' mumbled the scientist. 'Breaking in—too dangerous and silly,' he repeated, failing to sound surprised. How did Sophie know his exact plan? He dabbed his forehead with a hanky. 'That was plan A,' he admitted. He glanced back at the sleeping dog. 'But I'm not sure what plan B is, you see. If we have less than two days left to save GM451, I think it may be dangerous and silly to do anything other than break out this madman.' The professor ignored Ollie's gasp. 'The question is, how?'

Silence fell on the small crowd. Ben scratched his ear and the professor twirled his spectacles, deep in thought.

'We can do it,' woofed Star, standing on her hind legs and jabbing a paw into her chest to make herself understood. 'My bruv and I. We're spy pups, remember. We can access areas that adults and children can't. No person's ever broken in or out. But maybe two small, highly intelligent dogs can?'

'Brilliant idea, sis!' barked Spud, springing around the room in excitement. He especially liked the 'highly intelligent' bit. 'We find a way in, help break out Mr Big, get the antidote and then capture him again.'

The professor waved his hands to quieten the yapping puppies. 'Whatever's got into you two?' he frowned. 'Please calm down—we're trying to think of a plan to save your mother's life.'

'So are we,' yapped Star, leaping at the scientist.

Spud was already at the professor's laptop, pencil in mouth. He started to tap on the keys, woodpecker-style. 'Excuse the spelling mistakes,' he whined out of the side of his mouth.

Ben squinted at the screen and read out the words.

'"pupp£ to brake IN,"' he said aloud. '"help get big oUtt then save ma. MUSust catch bIG aga3in tho".'

Ben punched the air in delight. 'A

46

plan!' he yelled. 'Spud and Star have a plan to save Lara.' He high-fived the puppies.

Professor Cortex looked at the three children staring back at him, their eyes full of excitement. He stroked his chin and frowned while his mind whirred into action. 'Gadgets,' he nodded eventually. 'They'd need gadgets and a plan. And a map of the prison,' he said, enthusiasm growing in his voice.

The puppies yapped in joy. 'The prof says yes,' they woofed, chasing each other around the lab.

Spud danced on his hind legs, practising his punching and kicking. 'Take that, you baddie. And that,' he said, karate-chopping a nearby chair.

Sophie, Ollie and Ben hugged each other as Lara slept on.

The professor flicked open his phone and pressed a speed-dial button. He put his finger to his lips and the room fell quiet. 'Agent A,' he began. 'Yes, I'm sorry for waking you. Yes, of course it's an emergency! Life or death, in fact. Code Red. We may be about to lose one of our top spies. I need a favour, right now, if possible.'

Everyone listened carefully as the professor explained what he wanted.

9

BURNING METAL

Mr Big looked out of the window of his cell. It was the best room in the prison, with a luxury sea view. The only thing that ruined it was the sound of Archie and Gus snoring. He cursed as the lights went out and his flat screen TV went black. The usual footsteps came along the corridor outside.

A face appeared at the grille and, as always, the prison officer peered in. 'Nighty nighty, Mr Big. Sleep tight. See you at breakfast,' he snarled.

'Maybe you will,' replied the criminal. 'Or maybe I've eaten my last breakfast in this place,' he said under his breath.

*   *   *

The professor's laboratory was filled with tubes, beakers, potions and computers. Ollie slid his hands firmly into his pockets and they all followed the professor, Lara limping slowly behind them.

'OK,' he said. 'This is deadly serious stuff so you need to listen. We have one chance at breaking out His Evilness. The puppy agents will play the major role. GM451 is too ill to take part, so will stay with your parents. For the moment I'll tell them she's come down with something but I'm working on it.' *Not exactly a lie*, he thought, remembering how furious Mrs Cook had been with him in the past.

'And what about us?' asked Ollie, frowning at the professor.

'Yes, how can we help?' said Sophie.

The professor fiddled nervously with his spectacles. He avoided eye contact with Lara. 'The puppies are taking on most of the danger,' nodded the scientist. 'But my plan involves a minor role for you all too.'

Mrs Cook won't be pleased about that, thought Lara. *But what other option do I have?* 'Spud and Star,' she whimpered, 'make sure you don't put the kids in danger. Mr Big is the most evil baddie I've ever dealt with. He can't be trusted.'

'We won't, Mum,' said Star, licking her face affectionately. 'You've got enough to worry about.'

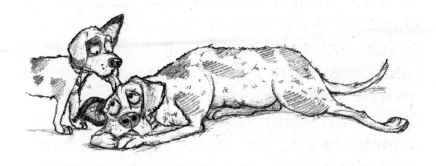

'What about gadgets?' asked Ben excitedly. 'Will we need some James Bond-type accessories?'

'You won't,' said the professor, shaking his head. 'Although you can all have GPS watches, now the neighbourhood pets have put them to the test. That way I can track you, and you can always find your way home. But Mr Big will need the serious stuff. Your job is to make sure he gets the resources he needs.'

'And what are they?' asked Sophie.

'Firstly,' said the professor, 'he'll need some of my home-made brain formula.'

'So he can out-think the guards! Great idea, Prof,' said Ben.

'Er, no, Benjamin,' explained the professor. 'I accidentally made a batch that was far too strong. It's actually rather dangerous. Watch this experiment.'

The scientist fixed goggles over his spectacles and waited for the children to put theirs on too. He took a small bottle of brain formula from his lab coat pocket and poured a few drops on to a sheet of metal. There was a fizzing sound and some red smoke as the liquid burnt right through.

'Iron,' explained the professor, holding it up and peering through the hole. 'Burnt through in seconds. This is the same metal that the prison bars are made of.'

'Cool,' cooed Ollie. 'So he can break out of his cell.'

The professor's mobile rang and he answered it. 'Hello, Agent A. Yes, I need the exact colour of the walls of Hurtmore Island maximum security prison. Of course it's a strange request,' he barked. 'And of course it's important I get the answer!' The professor's nostrils flared in frustration. He picked up a pencil and scribbled something on a pad before clicking his phone shut. 'Slate grey,' he said. 'Nice colour.'

The three children looked puzzled until Ben eventually asked, 'But according to your top-secret report his cell's on the seventh floor. How's he going to get down? And over the wall? And across the sea?'

'Trust me. Things will take shape,' soothed the professor.

Ollie danced with excitement. 'We're going to make this happen!' he said. Spud and Star jumped up and yapped away beside him.

'We'll save you, Mum!' agreed Spud.

The professor waited for calm. 'Right, everyone. We celebrate *after* we've pulled this off. Until then this is deadly serious.'

'So what's the plan?' asked Sophie, keen to hear what the professor had in mind.

'Good question.' The scientist took from his printer a piece of paper that contained a map of the prison grounds. 'The pups are going in,' he explained, 'and then entering the sewer at this point.' He tapped his finger at a spot on the diagram. 'I'll arrange for the power to be cut, which will give just enough time to get out of sight before the emergency generator kicks in. Before then, you, Ben and Ollie will have to visit Mr Big,' he explained. 'We need to get a message to him.'

'When are we breaking him out?' asked Ben, his eyes shining with excitement.

Professor Cortex looked at Lara, who did her best to look hopeful. 'As soon as possible, Benjamin. The spy pups are on their mission tomorrow night.'

10

PLANE CRAZY

'They call it Hurtmore Island,' explained Professor Cortex. 'It's classed as ultra-maximum high security,' he noted, as everyone looked at the map. He nodded at the computer screen. 'I've been researching. There have been four attempted escapes since it opened. One prisoner died falling off the roof; two were ripped to shreds by the guard dogs.'

Spud and Star looked at each other. *Guard dogs?*

'Only one man ever actually got over the wall,' continued the scientist.

'And what happened to him?' asked Ben.

'Drowned during the swim for freedom,' replied the professor gravely. 'The prison is a mile offshore and there's a very strong current. If that doesn't get you, the cold surely will.

'This looks like the entrance,' he continued, pointing at the drawing. 'It's

heavily guarded so there's absolutely no chance of getting in or out there. Agent A suggests the only possible exit is here,' he said, running his finger along a line that went from the main building to the wall. 'We'd need a plan to break him out. And a way of getting across the water, of course,' he added, scratching his bald head.

'So what about the pups and escaping prisoners?' asked Sophie. 'How will they get over?'

'This line, Sophie, is a sewer pipe

that runs underground. It goes right to the edge of the wall.'

Star and Spud wagged excitedly. 'We've explored tunnels before!' woofed Spud, thinking back to a recent holiday and their adventures with hidden treasure.

'And then there's a huge wall to get over,' Sophie pointed out. 'Followed by a mile swim! I guess nobody's ever escaped for a reason. It looks almost impossible!'

'Nothing's impossible, kids,' woofed Lara, dragging herself over to the professor and checking out the plan. *The question is, Prof: if the tunnel entrance is on the other side of the prison wall, how do you get in?*

11

A BIG VISIT

Mr Big heard the guard's footsteps outside and the clunk as his cell door was unlocked. The grille opened and a face peered through the gap.

'Wakey, wakey, rise and shine,' said the guard. 'Oh, and by the way, you've got some visitors.'

Mr Big smiled. He had no family or friends, at least none on the outside. Just acquaintances. And acquaintances never visited people in prison. *Must be part of the escape committee*, he thought to himself as he ran the tap to brush his teeth. He squeezed toothpaste on to his prison toothbrush, and looked into the mirror.

And I wonder if they'll recognize me, he grinned to himself. The master criminal had spent tens of thousands of pounds on plastic surgery to alter his image and it had been worthwhile. His bloated face had been replaced by a carefully chiselled film-star image and he took every opportunity to look in mirrors. He considered his ski-slope nose to be a masterpiece of cosmetic surgery. This handsome exterior cleverly masked his evil interior. Behind the sculptured cheekbones and wig was a cruel, calculating personality with evil running through his veins.

Mr Big finished brushing his teeth. He wiped his mouth and decided to skip breakfast. *Escape is on the menu.*

He heard the guard coming back to let him out of his cell. Dressed in his prison uniform Mr Big strolled to the visitors' area. The prison warden looked surprised to see him.

'Your first time down here,' he remarked, looking at his sheet. 'Seems your kids have turned up to see you.'

'My kids?' exclaimed the criminal. 'I don't hav— I mean . . . what brilliant news. My little darlings are here to see their long-lost dad. This should be fun.'

Mr Big was allocated a seat while his visitors were signed in. The door opened and there stood Ben, Sophie and Ollic. They looked around, trying

to find the horrible man who had tried
to kill their pet so many times. His evil
face was hard to forget.

'Where is he?' Ben whispered out of
the side of his mouth.

As the guard stood waiting for the
children to be reunited with their father,
Mr Big realized that his new look wasn't
helping the plan.

'Kids!' he gushed, and the three
Cook children turned to stare at him.
He was nothing like they remembered,
but all three recognized the same evil
look in his eyes. They felt sick to their
stomachs.

Ben took a deep breath. 'Father,' he
said, failing to sound genuine. 'We've

missed you so much. So good to see you.'

'Son?' exclaimed Mr Big, going along with the charade. 'How delightful to see you. And you've brought the other two with you.'

'Yes, Father, and you've *really changed* since we last saw you,' added Sophie.

Ben held his brother and sister by the hand and strolled forward. He knew the guards were watching and that CCTV would be recording their every move. There was no room for error. This was a crucial part of the escape plan and, if they failed, their pet would die.

'Give your old dad a hug,' beckoned the evil criminal.

Ben gave a reluctant bear hug. Sophie refused. Ollie hugged Mr Big and bit him at the same time.

'Ouch, you little horror,' he growled through gritted teeth. There was only one thing that Mr Big hated more than dogs and that was children.

'Now, now, Daddy,' smiled Ollie. 'You have to be nice to me, remember?' he said, deliberately stamping on the man's toe.

'Good to see you, kiddies,' lied Mr Big, holding Ollie at arm's length. 'How's the dog?'

Sophie burst into tears but Ben remained calm. 'She's not at her best, Father,' he said. 'But we've brought you a present.' He opened his backpack and pulled out a packet of biscuits.

'How thoughtful,' purred Mr Big. 'Custard creams!'

The guard came over to inspect the packet. Everyone went silent. He turned the packet over and decided there was nothing suspicious about an unopened packet of custard creams. The guard nodded and stood close by, listening in to the conversation.

Ben chatted away, trying to act natural, and Ollie chipped in with some childish nonsense.

'Time's nearly up, kiddies,' said the guard. 'Say goodbye to your daddy. He won't be home for a long, long time.'

'Eat them all at once and it'll spell trouble,' said Ben as the children turned to leave.

Ollie decided to try for one last bite, on behalf of Lara. He threw himself at

Mr Big and pretended to be upset. 'I can't leave you, Dad,' he yelled, his fists banging into the prisoner's stomach.

'Get off me, brat—I mean *son*,' said Mr Big, holding the boy as far away as possible.

Ollie kicked and screamed, feigning distress at being dragged away. Secretly he was pleased that he'd landed a few final good punches.

The children left the room and Mr Big picked up his biscuits. He wasn't sure what was going on but was certain that this was part of an escape plan.

12

PARACHUTE PUPS

Spud caught up with his sister, a star in name and shape as she fell through the night sky towards the earth. 'Pull the parachute cord after three!' he woofed.

Star's cheeks billowed as she reached for the ripcord and caught it in her mouth. But the puppies were falling fast and she panicked and let go of it.

The wind was blowing Spud's lips apart so his fangs were showing and his eyes were watering. *Stay calm*, he told himself as the twinkling lights of the prison got closer. He grabbed his own ripcord and held it between his teeth. *Like this*, he pointed as his sister turned to have another go. 'Excellent,' he woofed out of the side of his mouth. 'After three. One . . . two . . . and three . . .'

The puppies pulled their ripcords together and both parachutes exploded from their backpacks. The freefall was slowed and Star calmed down a little.

'Check the view,' woofed Spud, pointing below. 'That's the prison,' he said, tugging another cord that swung him left a little. He certainly didn't want to end up in the ocean! 'We need to land just inside the perimeter wall.' Spud looked at his GPS watch from Professor Cortex, the luminous dial ticking towards midnight. 'Any second n—' he began as the prison below was plunged into darkness.

'That's the professor's team cutting

the electricity,' yelled Spud. 'We have one minute and forty-three seconds until the emergency lighting kicks in.'

The spy pups glided safely down into the grounds of the maximum security prison, unhooked their parachutes and dragged them to a manhole cover. It was just where the professor's map had said it would be. The moon came out from behind a cloud, providing some light.

Spud checked his watch. *Yikes! Twenty seconds to go*. He and his sister levered their claws under the metal rim. 'It sure is heavy,' he whined. The lid shifted a little but not enough to get in. 'Heave ho, sis,' he panted. 'This is going to be a close call.' *Ten . . . nine . . . eight . . .*

The lid finally popped and Star disappeared inside just as the emergency generator whirred into action and the lights came on. Spud crouched down, absolutely still. The manhole cover was half off as his sister pulled the parachutes inside. A beam of light was swinging his way. *Quick, sis*, he thought, *before I'm discovered.*

The final parachute went through the gap and Spud's

back legs and tail disappeared just as the searchlight fell on the manhole cover.

'What's that?' asked the guard from the watchtower. 'Some movement in no-man's-land. At that manhole.'

'Where?' asked his mate, pointing his binoculars towards it.

As the searchlight swept away, Spud and Star pushed up their heads and heaved the manhole cover closed above them.

'Looked like a small animal. Back legs disappeared down the hole,' said the guard.

'Oh,' laughed his mate. 'I thought you'd seen someone escaping.' They watched as the searchlight went back over the manhole. It was shut tight. 'Looks fine over there. Warn me if you see something getting out,' he said, 'but breaking into this place would be just plain stupid. Besides, that manhole leads to the sewer. You'd have to be crazy to go down there.'

* * *

The two crazy spy puppies crouched in the tunnel. 'Close one!' woofed Spud. 'But don't worry, sis,' he reassured, 'that's the hard part done with.'

Star was trembling with fear. The tunnel was eerie but certainly safer than jumping from an aeroplane. 'Let wag-power shine the way,' she said. They were grateful for the professor's inventions. Sometimes things didn't work out but the wag-powered torches, attached to their helmets, were one of his better ideas.

Star managed a shaky wag and her torch lit up the tunnel. Spud's confident wag doubled the brightness and they scanned the area.

'Phooey,' woofed Star, 'what a stink.'

The pups checked each other's backpacks. The professor needed one of these delivered to Mr Big as a matter of urgency. If they failed, their mum would die. The puppies turned and began to trot towards the main prison building.

'No time to waste,' reminded Star. 'We have to be in place by nine.'

13

BISCUIT BRAINS

Mr Big got back to his cell and thought about what the children had said. *There must be a code in there somewhere*, he thought, replaying the encounter in his mind. He flicked on the kettle and made a cup of Earl Grey tea. Being the scariest prisoner had a few perks, like the guards ignoring some of his luxuries.

He glanced at the packet of biscuits. Maybe it was them? Surely the children weren't stupid enough to think he would eat biscuits, not after he'd used poisoned custard creams to disable the dog. 'If you eat them all at once, it'll spell trouble,' he said aloud. Mr Big opened the packet and took a biscuit. 'Spell trouble?' He checked it closely and saw it had a letter etched in it. 'P,' he said, quickly opening the packet and turning all the biscuits over to reveal letters. 'It's like Scrabble.'

The door opened and Archie

scampered into the cell, closely followed by the lumbering frame of Gus, both back from breakfast. Mr Big flicked on the kettle again and made two more cups, this time of builder's tea.

'Biscuits,' exclaimed Gus, stuffing a custard cream into his mouth.

Mr Big turned, spilling hot tea on his leg. 'Stop that, you idiot!' he yelled, grabbing Gus's mouth and yanking it open. 'They're coded biscuits. Don't swallow!' he instructed as Gus choked up the half-eaten custard cream.

'Too late, boss,' he coughed. 'But I only scoffed one. You've still got plenty left,' he pointed, hoping he would be forgiven.

Mr Big pieced the soggy biscuit back together. 'Looks like a "g"—or a "6". Let's hope you've not eaten a vital part of the clue,' raged Mr Big, rearranging the biscuits into alphabetical order. 'I've just had a visit from some horrible brats who are part of our escape plan. They gave me these coded biscuits. We just need to work out the message. And one of the blighters gave me a nasty nip,' he said, showing the teeth marks to his cellmates.

'Ouch,' soothed Archie.

Mr Big hated being bitten. He remembered his first encounter with that dratted spy dog. She'd chased him through a forest and sunk her teeth into his backside. Then she'd held on until the police arrived. The criminal felt his bottom, gingerly running his fingers over the teeth marks. *Children and dogs*, he shivered. *Yuck!*

Archie was busy spelling words with the biscuits. 'Nineteen biccies, boss,' he said. 'Twenty counting the one Gus scoffed.'

Mr Big glared and the hulking man looked down at his feet.

'Some letters, symbols and numbers,' Archie added.

Archie and Mr Big sipped their tea while Gus paced up and down like an expectant father. He was an old-fashioned criminal—short on brains but heavy on brawn. He couldn't spell 'punch' but he could throw one all right.

Twenty minutes later they'd agreed on the message. 'What does it say?' asked Gus, peering at the table.

'*Gym then showers at 9.30 p.m.*,' growled Mr Big.

'Or *showers then gym at 9.30 p.m.*,' added Archie stupidly. 'But I think the boss is right.'

Mr Big checked his watch. 'It's 10 a.m. Get your kit ready, boys,' he purred. 'You look like you need a workout.'

*   *   *

The professor had ordered a Secret Service van kitted out with the latest spy technology. He watched as the dots moved towards the centre of the screen. 'They're making good headway,' he nodded to himself.

73

Lara was asleep on the sofabed. He was pleased to see her tummy rising as she breathed in and out but was concerned that her chest was rattling.

The scientist put a stethoscope to the sleeping dog's chest. 'Her condition is worsening by the minute,' he said gravely. 'I just hope we can pull this off in time.'

*   *   *

Star and Spud paddled through the tunnel. 'Not pleasant,' yapped Star, trying not to think of what she was treading in. Both puppies' tails were on full wag, their torches cutting through the eerie blackness.

'Come in, agents,' said a voice in Star's ear. 'Are you receiving?'

Star gave a single bark for 'yes'.

'Excellent,' said the professor. 'Are you at the junction yet?'

Two woofs.

'OK,' said the professor, pointing to the red dots on the screen. 'We see you. Fifty metres ahead, you take the left tunnel. Then upwards to the grille.

Then wait. He should be there at half nine.'

Someone flushed a toilet in the prison and a surge of water swelled towards the puppies. 'Poo alert!' woofed Spud as he scrambled to the side, avoiding the smelly water. Star was too slow and the tidal wave hit her head on, drenching her in sewage.

'Sorry, sis,' he woofed, holding a paw and hauling her out of the sludge.

It was a horrible ordeal. But definitely not as horrible as what their mum was going through. They simply couldn't let her die without trying to save her. Even if it meant carrying out one of the professor's most hare-brained plans yet.

Star shook her body and carried on walking.

14

GYM'LL FIX IT

The prison guard sat nervously outside the governor's office. He felt like a naughty schoolchild waiting to be summoned by the head teacher. He flicked through a copy of *Prison Monthly* until eventually the sign on the door went green and he knocked gingerly.

'Come,' bellowed a voice from within. The prison guard entered the huge office. The governor was leaning back in a leather chair, hands clasped in front of his chest.

'Wilcox,' he beamed, standing to greet the officer. 'How good of you to see me.'

Wilcox managed a watery smile before perching on a chair. 'Good of you to invite me, sir,' he stammered. He'd worked at the prison for thirteen years and had never met the governor before.

'As you know, Wilcox, nobody's ever escaped from this prison.'

'Yes, sir,' agreed the officer. 'Although a few have tried,' he smiled.

'And failed,' finished the governor with a satisfied grin. 'My next promotion rests on us continuing that outstanding record,' he nodded. 'Which is why I want you to tell me about Big.'

'Big, sir?'

'Yes, Big, sir,' agreed the governor. 'I'm hearing strange noises on the grapevine.'

'Strange noises, sir? Well, he did hand a laptop in the other day, sir,' volunteered the officer. 'Which is kind of unusual for a thug of his stature.'

The governor cocked his head on one side and put his hands together as if praying.

'And he had some visitors this morning, sir,' continued Wilcox, gaining in confidence. 'His first ones ever.'

'And who were they?' enquired the governor, deep in concentration.

'His kids, sir,' nodded the guard.

'His kids, sir,' nodded the chief. 'Interesting. What if I was to tell you, Wilcox, that Big doesn't have any children?'

The guard's eyes widened. 'But there were three of them, sir. Brought him some biscuits and everything.'

The prison governor was paid to be calm. 'Something's going on, Wilcox,' he soothed. 'I would like our friend Mr Big brought here to chat to me, please.'

'Of course, sir. When?'

'Right now!' spat the governor, his anger spilling over.

'Yes, sir,' said the guard. 'I saw him heading for the gym. I'll go and get him right away.'

*   *   *

Mr Big hated the gym. He did a bit of cycling while Archie scampered on the treadmill and Gus lifted huge weights. At 9.25 he picked up his towel and headed for the changing room.

'What now, boss?' asked Gus as the three men sat down and waited. He pulled off his sweaty socks and began to get changed back into his prison uniform.

Mr Big scanned the room. There was a shower area and hundreds of lockers. He wasn't quite sure what he was supposed to do. 'The biscuit code said be here at half nine. We wait.'

In the corner of the room Spud peered out from a vent at the base of the lockers. 'Not sure which one he is,' whined the puppy to his sister. 'The prof never had time to show us a picture.'

'There's only one way to recognize him,' reminded Star. 'Remember what Mum told us? About biting his bottom. Find the bloke with the scarred bum and we have our man.'

The puppies waited patiently. They watched as men came and went. A huge man took off his socks and Star nearly fainted. 'Phooey,' she whispered as the cheesy smell wafted across the changing room. His pants came down and they examined his bottom. 'No teeth marks.'

A man with film-star features wandered into the shower, with a towel round him, so neither puppy could get a decent look at his rump. There was more waiting as the man stopped to look in every mirror before he showered and dried himself. It was now 9.45.

'It has to be him,' whined Spud. The man lowered his towel and turned to put his pants on. 'Hairy bottom,' woofed Spud, 'with teeth marks! Bingo! That's our target.' He pushed against the vent cover and the puppies emerged from their hiding place.

'Let's go, bro!' woofed Star.

'Boss, there's a d-dog,' pointed Archie as the pair of pups scampered across the tiled floor.

Mr Big grinned. 'Pooches,' he growled. 'So good to see you. You must be related to Spy Dog. Tell me, little

mutts, how is your dear old ma?' The criminal reached into a locker and pulled out a small bottle containing the antidote. He grinned, and waved it in front of the puppies.

Spud bared his teeth in his fiercest growl. 'How do you think she is, you evil man! My sister and I hate you for what you've done. Sure, we're going to help you escape but once we've got the antidote, you can be sure we'll come after you.'

'What's the plan, little pooches?' asked Mr Big, pulling on his prison clothes and securing the bottle in his jacket pocket.

Star shrugged off her backpack and hurled it at the man. 'In there,' she growled. 'Everything you need, including instructions. Read it. Do it. We're breaking you out of here tonight.'

The changing-room door opened and in walked two prison officers. They scanned the room, looking for Mr Big.

'*Yikes!*' whined Spud, hiding behind Archie's hairy legs.

One of the guards spotted Mr Big. 'The governor wants to see you,' he shouted. 'Pronto.'

Star and Spud sprinted for their escape route. 'Job done. Back down to the sewer, sis,' yapped Spud as he squeezed through the vent and shoved his sister down towards the drain.

15

THE TWITS

The prison governor beckoned Mr Big into his office. 'Good of me to see you,' he smiled. 'Take a seat.'

The evil criminal sat gingerly. He placed the small backpack on his knee, clutching it tightly. He wasn't sure what was in the bag but he knew it was crucial to his escape. 'What's all this about, sir?' asked Mr Big in his best innocent voice. He was calm on the outside but could feel panic bubbling on the inside.

'You tell me, Big,' snapped the governor. 'First we have the laptop episode—your first ever good deed. Then we have your first ever visit. By children you don't even have. And now your first ever trip to the gym.'

The men stared at each other until the prison boss blinked. 'That's a lot of firsts,' he concluded.

'New leaf, sir,' lied Mr Big. 'I've

learnt from my mistakes,' he continued, delivering another whopper.

The governor looked at the backpack. The criminal was gripping it so tightly that his knuckles were white. Something wasn't right. 'You know escape is impossible,' noted the boss. 'Four have tried,' he said, eyeing the backpack, 'and four have died.'

'I'd be a fool to even try,' agreed Mr Big.

'Quite. So what's in the bag?' enquired the governor, holding out his hand.

Mr Big pulled the bag closer, his knuckles clenched. He was so close to freedom. If the governor peeped in at his escape kit he was doomed.

'Gym kit, sir,' he replied, delivering his third lie in less than a minute.

'Then you won't mind if I take a look,' soothed the prison governor.

Mr Big's face twitched. A million things ran through his mind, including the fact that very soon the governor might be the fifth one to die. 'You can look in the bag if you want to,' said the criminal. 'But I'd strongly advise that you don't.'

'And why not?' asked the prison boss, taking the backpack and unzipping it.

'Because it could be bad for your health,' snarled the criminal in his first honest remark of the conversation. Mr Big was breathing heavily. The bag was wide open and he could see some grey material inside. And a note.

The governor raised his head and stared at Mr Big. 'My health?' he frowned. 'Are you threatening me?'

'Not exactly, sir,' stammered the criminal, his bravado turning to simmering panic. 'I mean, the bag contains my sweaty gym kit. Including socks,' he said. 'And Gus's pants,' he blurted. 'Used!'

The governor winced. This was a serious health warning. Both men jumped as the phone rang and the governor took an urgent call. Mr Big breathed a sigh of relief as he was shooed away, grabbing the pups' backpack on the way.

*   *   *

Archie and Gus got to work on the sheets, tying them together to make a rope. Mr Big shook the bars on the window. 'Loose,' he smiled. 'The prof's formula is working a treat.' He squirted a few more drops at the bars and stood back as the metal fizzed. He wafted away the fumes as Gus pulled at a bar.

Gus's gold teeth glinted in the moonlight as the bar came away in his hands. After ten minutes the bars were history. Mr Big had consulted the instructions several times. One bar was left intact and the sheet rope tied to it. Mr Big checked the instructions once more and then folded the note and placed it securely in his pocket.

'What does it say, boss?' whined Gus.

'Top secret,' he said. 'If I told you, I'd have to kill you,' he added truthfully. 'And you can't read anyway, remember? All you need to know is that Archie's first out, then you. We just have to wait for the signal.'

'What's the signal?' asked Gus, punching the wall in preparation for fighting the guards later on.

'That,' said Mr Big, cupping his ear. 'Right on cue.'

The men strained to listen. Below in the yard came the sound of three puppy barks.

The yapping stopped and Archie was first down the sheet rope. He swung effortlessly, as if he were half man, half monkey. Once he'd landed in the yard he pulled three times on the home-made rope.

'Me next?' asked Gus.

Just as he was about to nod, Mr Big noticed a searchlight sweeping towards them. If the white sheets were left dangling they'd be discovered! He hauled at the rope, pulling it upwards as fast as he could.

Gus spotted the light too and together they yankcd the sheets through the window and ducked from view just as the beam scanned their cell. Neither criminal breathed for a minute.

Mr Big peered out again to check that the light was gone, and threw the makeshift rope out. Gus tugged on it and looked down. If Archie was a monkey, Gus was a silverback gorilla. He looked unsure.

'Go on, Gussy,' soothed Mr Big. 'I'll be right behind you.'

Gus took a deep breath and climbed out of the window. He held on to the sheets and lowered himself down. But when he was halfway, there was a ripping sound. Mr Big heard a *'Yikes!'* and then a big *rip* and heavy *thud* as the man hit the dirt floor. There was some scuffling as Archie and Gus sank into the shadows, Gus whimpering about his broken ankle.

'Shush, you idiots,' hissed Mr Big from above. Then he hauled the remaining sheets back into the cell. Now he had no chance of escape. Luckily, he wasn't scheduled to go down the rope anyway. He checked the note once more.

Mr Big pulled the bits from the puppy backpack and slipped off his prison uniform. He pulled on the slate-grey clothes and applied the grey face pack and hairspray. Then he slipped the antidote into his top pocket. He checked the mirror and smiled. 'Slate grey from head to foot. I look like one of those human statues,' he grinned. 'But now for the difficult part.'

The evil criminal reached into the backpack and pulled out the professor's latest invention. The moon came out from behind a cloud and he squinted at the scribbled diagram. 'I hope you know what you're doing, old man,' he muttered under his breath. 'Your dog's life depends on it.'

Mr Big fiddled with the gadgets for a while before making his way to the bar-less window. He dropped a stone to signal phase two. 'Go, boys, go,' he smirked.

Gus and Archie didn't know it but they were the decoys. They were also doomed. Mr Big loved double-crossing people and this was going exactly to plan.

'There's the pebble,' woofed Spud, his ears on red alert. Down below Mr Big's cell, the puppies coaxed Archie and Gus out of the shadows.

'This way to the front gate,' woofed Star quietly. 'Follow us out here, guys.'

'That's a lot of woofing, doggies,' sobbed Gus, limping badly. 'What are we supposed to do? Follow you? There're guards everywhere.'

'Yeah, and Big isn't going to be happy that we left him behind,' Archie added nervously.

They shrank behind a barrel as another searchlight cut through the darkness.

'A few more steps,' urged Star. 'Just a teeny bit further.'

Archie was propping up his huge friend as Gus dragged his broken foot behind him. They were both out in the open, darkness their only cover. The next searchlight came their way and the men fell to the ground. But Star and Spud stood tall and waved at the tower.

'Cooee!' woofed Spud in his loudest

91

bark. 'We have two escapees here!'

The light swept across them and then doubled back in search of the noise.

'What are you doing, dog?' said Gus, grabbing on to Archie even more tightly.

Spud stood proudly in the prison yard, the spotlight picking him out like a lead singer on stage. He stood on his hind legs and barked his best bark. 'Wakey, wakey, everyone,' he woofed. 'We're escaping. Let the action begin!'

A siren sounded as the prison officer hit the emergency button.

Archie tried to run for it but Gus wouldn't let go and they both collapsed in a heap. All the other watchtowers focused their lights on the area as the two criminals stood up, blinded by the glare.

'Put your hands on your heads,' came a voice from a loudspeaker. 'One false move and we shoot.'

Gus fell back to the floor in floods of tears, one hand in the air and one hand clutching his ankle. 'I've broken something,' he sobbed. 'I want my mum.'

Archie's life sentence stretched before

him and, with Gus no longer hanging on to him, he started running. Bullets thudded into the ground and he ran faster, zigzagging towards the prison wall. But when he reached it he realized there was nowhere left to run. He turned and raised his hands, squinting into the dazzling searchlights. 'Don't shoot!' he panted. 'We'll tell you everything.'

A van pulled up and men with snarling guard dogs emerged.

'*Yikes!*' woofed Spud. 'I don't like the look of them. Let's scoot.'

Star knew the plan off by heart. She guided her brother through the shadows towards the prison's kitchen door and leapt into the skip outside. 'We leave first thing in the morning,' she woofed. 'With the trash.'

Spud bounced into the skip. 'Mmm,' he woofed, 'leftover food. This is the best plan ever!'

16

OVER AND OUT

The governor was woken by the phone ringing. 'Yes,' he croaked. 'Captured? When?' He sat up and switched on the bedside lamp. It was 2 a.m. 'Who have you got?' He leapt out of bed and attempted to get dressed while still on the phone. 'What about their pal, Mr Big?' he asked. 'I want his cell checked,' he shouted, holding the phone in place with his shoulder while he poked his feet into his pants. 'I'm on my way.'

*　　*　　*

Mr Big leant out of his cell window to check what was going on. 'Exactly as it says on the note,' he purred. 'All the attention is on those two idiots while I just slip away.'

The master criminal sat on the window ledge and looked at the view. It was the dead of night. Clouds were scudding across the sky and he could see the prison wall. Beyond that was blackness. *The sea!* And beyond that some twinkling lights. *Freedom!*

'Here goes,' he told himself as he swung out of his cell and threw his hand at the wall. There was a squelch as the sucker stuck. A foot followed, then his other hand and foot until he was hanging seven storeys up. He unsucked a hand and moved it down. Then a foot. Slowly but surely he was crawling, lizard-like, down the prison wall. The professor's invention was working perfectly.

Mr Big was almost at the bottom when a searchlight came his way. Archie and Gus had been captured and the guards were now back to routine checks. Mr Big froze as the powerful beam scanned the wall and moved slowly across his body. His slate-grey outfit blended in and he breathed a sigh of relief as the light kept sweeping.

He jumped the last few feet and dusted himself off in preparation for the next move. This had to be perfectly timed. Mr Big faced a thirty-metre sprint across no-man's-land towards the external wall. The professor's note had said this was the riskiest part.

Mr Big waited for another sweep of the beam before making a dash for it. He reached the external wall and leapt as high as he could, suckering himself like a lizard once more. This time it was upwards. His breathing was heavy as he squelched to the top, stopping once more to let the light sweep over his slate-grey suit. He cursed as he cut himself on the glass on the top of the wall.

He looked out at the free world just as a platform was being raised from a cherry-picker vehicle below. Professor Cortex smiled grimly and offered his hand as Mr Big jumped off the wall. The professor pushed a button and the platform was lowered to the ground and, for one evil criminal, to freedom.

*　　*　　*

This was the professor's first ever true crime. Mr Big stood opposite him, and if he was counting he'd know that escaping from maximum security prison was his seven hundred and ninety-third offence in a life devoted to crime. In the good-versus-evil battle, the professor was a novice. He didn't stand a chance.

'We've kept our part of the deal,' noted the professor, his voice wavering slightly.

'That's very noble of you,' sneered the one-man crime wave. 'Nearly didn't make it, though. I had a very uncomfortable moment with the governor.'

'We broke you out. Now we need the antidote. GM451 is very ill. We may already be too late.'

'Deary me,' said Mr Big. 'How dreadfully sad.' He reached into his top pocket and pulled out a small bottle of purple liquid. Professor Cortex reached for it and Mr Big withdrew his arm. 'Not so fast, old man,' he snarled. 'If that dog recovers, then there's only one thing she'll focus on. And that's catching me. I'll be much safer with her out of the way, thanks very much.'

Professor Cortex reached for his mobile. 'I'll c-call the p-police,' he stammered.

Mr Big's plastic face stretched into an uncomfortable grin. He reached into his jacket and pulled out one of the iron bars from his cell window.

The professor was terrible at crime. With one menacing look from Mr Big he handed over the mobile before being ushered into the cherry picker. Mr Big pressed the button that lifted the scientist back up as high as the prison wall.

The scientist looked over into the prison and cringed at the chaos he'd caused. All the courtyard lights were on as prison officers rushed about, their guard dogs yapping and sirens blaring. He looked back at Mr Big, far below.

'Bye bye.' The criminal waved to the stricken scientist. 'I'll be sure to send you a postcard from Brazil.'

Mr Big stumbled towards the shoreline, looking for the professor's boat. 'No way,' he said, slapping his head in frustration. A black pedalo had been pulled up the shore. 'That's his escape vehicle?' But Mr Big had no time to lose. He heaved the pedalo to the water and scrambled in. His legs started pumping. The sea may be black but freedom shone brightly in the distance. He headed for the lights on the far shore, a part of him regretting he'd not been a regular at the prison gym.

17

BIG TROUBLE

The head of MI5 had been summoned from her bed. The professor stared down at his shoes. The Cook children looked ashamed and the puppies cowered underneath Ben and Sophie's legs. Mr Cook wiped the sleep from his eyes and Mrs Cook was wearing one of her sternest looks.

'How could you, Maximus?' yelled the MI5 chief. 'What on earth were you thinking?'

'The plan was—'

'Whatever the plan was,' bellowed the

lady, 'it's resulted in an escaped prisoner. A very dangerous escaped prisoner,' she reminded him. 'And you *planned* his escape!'

Ollie was marvelling at the veins in the lady's neck. He'd never seen veins stick out so much.

'You actually *helped* him over the wall! And *provided* him with an escape boat.'

'Pedalo,' piped up Ollie.

'And as for you lot,' she continued, walking the line. 'Don't think you'll get off scot-free.' She held up a photograph of the children hugging Mr Big. Mrs Cook stifled a shriek as the spy boss continued. 'This is a very serious offence indeed. Aiding and abetting an escapee from a maximum security prison.' She paused to calm down but couldn't. 'I can hardly think of a worse crime!' she exploded. 'What on earth am I going to tell the Prime Minister?'

'That our dog's ill,' suggested Ben bravely. 'And breaking out Mr Big was our only chance.'

'And now that chance seems to have

gone,' sobbed Sophie. 'And Lara will die.'

Star and Spud hung their heads. It was bad enough that Mr Big had escaped. But that he'd double-crossed them and taken the antidote with him was even harder to bear.

Star checked her watch. She knew her mum was now desperately ill. It was 8 a.m. Lara had a maximum of four hours to live.

*   *   *

The family returned home in subdued mood. Lara followed in a pet ambulance and was stretchered into the lounge. She lay on the floor, her breathing difficult and her nose bone dry.

'Come on, kids,' said Mr Cook. 'Your mum and I don't agree with what you did but we understand why you did it.' All eyes fell on Lara. 'There's nothing you can do. We've been up all night.' He smiled. 'Let's get some sleep.'

The children volunteered to bed down in the lounge with their beloved pet. Ben and Sophie went nose to toe on the sofa and Ollie curled up on the chair. Star and Spud snuggled up to their poorly mum. Silence fell on the room as everyone slept. The clock seemed to tick louder than normal, a deadly reminder that Lara's life was slipping away.

At 9 a.m. Ben was woken by a text message. His bleary eyes checked it and he sat upright. 'Can't let GM die. Already in big trouble. Fancy more? Only u + pups outside now.'

Ben shook his sister and brother awake. 'The prof wants me to help him,' he croaked. 'I think he's got another plan. I'm taking the puppies. I need you to cover for me.'

'No way,' said Sophie. 'I'm coming too.'

'You can't. It's too dangerous,' Ben replied. 'Just cover, OK?'

Sophie looked at the sleeping dog. 'OK,' she agreed.

'Is this another spy-pup mission?' asked Ollie excitedly.

Spud and Star wagged furiously.

Who dares wins, panted Star.

Ben grabbed his backpack and slipped quietly out of the front door.

104

Sophie and Ollie watched from the window as Ben and the puppies got into the professor's van. It pulled away slowly and quietly. Sophie checked the clock and then Lara. Three hours and counting.

Once away from the house the professor put his foot down and the van accelerated noisily. 'What's up, Prof?' woofed Star. 'What's the plan?'

'OK, Ben,' said the scientist, 'here's the deal. I'm already in the biggest trouble I've ever been in, and that's before I speak to your mother properly. I'm facing disciplinary measures. Possibly even the sack. Maybe a stint in prison myself,' he winced. 'Breaking that evil man out of prison was a stupid thing to do. But we can't just let GM451 die. She's my life's work. I . . .' he began. 'I . . . I love her. There, I've said it. Prison or no prison, I owe it to GM451 to give it my best shot.'

'So what are we going to do?' asked Ben.

The puppies' tails were wagging furiously. They liked the professor's fighting spirit.

'I know I did some very stupid things last night, but I did have one success. Before Big escaped in the pedalo,' he explained, 'I planted a bugging device on him.' The professor pressed a button and his dashboard lit up. 'That dot is the evil man. Remember his last words to me? About Brazil? He's heading for the airport. And we're going to track him down and get the

106

antidote off him. We still have a few hours to save GM451 and I'm going to give it my all.'

'Will it be dangerous?' asked Ben, his heart pounding.

'One hundred per cent,' said the professor, taking his eyes off the road for a second and casting a glance at Ben and the pups. 'Are you up for it?'

The puppies' tongues lolloped out and their eyes shone. 'Never been more up for anything in my entire life!' woofed Star.

'Agent Spud reporting for duty,' wagged her brother.

Ben looked at the puppies and took a deep breath. 'A hundred per cent danger,' he said. 'Bring it on!'

18

ALL ABOARD

The professor's van pulled up outside the perimeter of the airfield. It was a relatively minor airport with a cabin for an office and one thin strip of tarmac. Within the fence they could see a few small planes. They watched as Mr Big emerged from a car and marched into the tiny airport office. 'Probably hiring a plane to take him abroad,' guessed the professor. 'Let's call the police.'

'Too late,' said Ben, pointing into the distance. Professor Cortex put the binoculars to his eyes and watched as the criminal marched up to a small aeroplane and hauled open the door. He threw in a bag and then shut the door again. A lorry lumbered out of an airport garage and pulled up at the plane. Mr Big and the lorry driver spoke for a few seconds before the escapee went back towards the office and the driver began refuelling the plane.

'Here's our chance,' said the professor. 'We've got a few minutes while he refuels. Then he'll be taking off. We have to get the puppies on to that plane so we can stop him before he leaves.'

Spud punched the air in delight. 'What an adventure,' he whooped. 'Being a spy pup is the best thing ever!'

'Calm down, bro,' barked Star. 'We've got a lot of thinking to do. We need to work out how to get on that plane without Mr Big or the lorry driver seeing us.'

The professor put the binoculars to his eyes and scanned the airfield again. He could see Mr Big buying a coffee from a machine. 'It's now or never,' he said. 'This is our moment, pups,' he gulped. 'No,' he corrected, 'this is your *mum*'s moment. We just need to get you on the other side of this fence.'

'I'll help,' suggested Ben. 'I can put the pups on leads and pretend to be walking them. I can get through the fence and accidentally wander on to the airfield. If anyone tells me off, I'll just pretend I didn't know.'

'And when we get close enough you can open the plane door, let us off our leads, we can scamper on to the plane —and get the antidote!' woofed Spud. 'It's perfect.'

'Not quite perfect,' corrected his sister. 'But probably the best we can do in the limited time we have.'

The professor was reluctant. He was already in massive trouble. Getting Ben involved in more danger was just digging him into an even bigger hole. 'It's a risk,' he said aloud.

'But the pups will be on the plane, not me,' pleaded Ben. 'And they're trained agents, so if anyone can stop Mr Big they can.'

There was a moment's silence, broken only by the thumping of Spud's tail. 'OK,' agreed the professor. 'Go, go, go!'

* * *

Mrs Cook peered into the lounge to check on Lara. 'Where's Ben?' she asked. 'And the puppies?' Sophie pretended to be asleep. Mum touched

110

Sophie on the shoulder to wake her. Sophie yawned and stretched. 'Where's your brother and Star and Spud?' she asked, this time a little more seriously.

'They couldn't sleep,' said Sophie. 'So Ben took them for walkies.'

'Oh,' said Mrs Cook, relaxing a little. 'Where did they go?'

'Not sure,' replied Sophie truthfully. 'But I'm sure they'll be back soon,' she said hopefully.

*　　*　　*

Professor Cortex took some wire cutters from the back of his van and

handed them to Ben. The boy walked the puppies casually along the side of the perimeter fence then, as they pretended to have a toilet stop, he bent down to cut a small hole in the wire. He pulled the wire back and squeezed through, getting his backpack caught in the process. Star grabbed it with her teeth and unhooked it, then the puppies scampered through, their tails swishing excitedly. Ben picked up their leads and they dragged him along, noses to the grass.

They walked past *Trespassers will be prosecuted* and *Beware of the dogs* signs.

Star gulped. 'The dogs on the picture sure look big and scary.'

'We're trained in martial arts,' reminded her brother. 'Mum's passed on her knowledge. I hope those dogs don't pick on us, for *their* sake!'

Ben watched from a distance as the tanker driver removed the hose from the plane. He jumped into his cab and the lorry trundled back to base. Time was running out. Ben led the puppies towards the small aircraft, then crouched down and let them off their leads. He felt around in his backpack as his mobile vibrated. 'Yes,' he whispered, ducking behind one of the wings.

'He's coming,' hissed Professor Cortex, nearly dropping his binoculars in alarm. He watched from afar as Mr Big strode from the office towards the now refuelled plane. 'Benjamin, get the dogs into the plane and make your escape.'

Ben peered round the wing and lay flat. He pointed in the direction of Mr Big to alert the pups. Then he reached for the aeroplane door and yanked it open. The puppies jumped aboard.

Professor Cortex watched in horror as the most evil criminal in the world strode straight towards Ben's hiding place. *A distraction*, he thought. *What can I do?*

'Over here,' yelled the professor. 'I say, is that you, Mr Big?' he shouted, frantically waving his arms to attract the man's attention.

Mr Big saw the professor and cursed. 'Not you again, old man,' he shouted, scanning the airfield, relieved to see there were no police cars. 'Well, you're too late this time,' he said, breaking

113

into a sprint towards the plane. 'Me and the antidote are up, up and away.'

'We'll catch you, you cold calculating evil criminal,' yelled the professor, pink with rage and shaking with fear.

'This is no time for compliments,' yelled Mr Big as he reached the aircraft and hauled the door open.

The professor watched with bated breath as the baddie swung himself into the pilot's seat and the engine spluttered into action. The propellers whirred and the plane taxied towards the runway.

'Phew,' breathed the professor, waiting to see Ben spring up from his hiding place. He scanned with the binoculars once more. 'Where are you, Benjamin?' he muttered.

The plane picked up speed and soon Mr Big was away. He arced the plane towards Professor Cortex and saluted as he flew over the old man. All the professor could do was stare in shock as he saw Ben's frightened face peering out from the back window.

19

MAYDAY

Ben lay on the back seat of the small aircraft, hidden beneath a blanket. The puppies were hiding underneath the passenger seat.

'Bye-bye, old fella,' they heard Mr Big say as he waved to Professor Cortex. 'I'll send you a postcard from Brazil!'

Ben felt the plane gathering height before it levelled off. The twin engines droned as Mr Big set his course. After a few minutes Ben was brave enough to poke his face out from underneath the blanket. He could see Star wagging excitedly. He followed her jabbing paw and Ben could see a small bottle of purple liquid poking out of Mr Big's jacket pocket.

The antidote, he realized. *After five*, he signalled to Star, holding his fingers up and counting down. *5 . . . 4 . . . 3 . . . 2 . . . 1* 'Go!' yelled Ben, startling Mr Big as he jumped up from the back seat.

Star snapped at his coat and the bottle fell out. Mr Big leapt from the pilot's seat, knocking the controls and throwing the plane into a nosedive. The criminal and Ben tangled in a heap as the engines whined and the plane twirled dangerously.

'Got it,' woofed Spud out of the side of his mouth, emerging from the chaos with the bottle clenched in his teeth. 'I've got the antidote!'

Mr Big leapt at the puppy and

snatched the bottle from his jaws. 'I'll take that back,' he sneered.

Star was sitting in the pilot's seat trying to steady the plane. She hit the controls with her paw and the aeroplane dived to the left. Everyone fell around the cabin and Mr Big's arm smashed against the window. Star sank her razor-sharp teeth into his arm. Mr Big yelled in pain and dropped the antidote. The bottle rolled under a seat and Ben grabbed it.

'Advantage puppies,' Spud woofed, out of kicking distance.

The criminal flared his nostrils. Star sat close by in the pilot's seat, baring her teeth and doing her nastiest growl. 'Tangle with me and you'll have more teeth marks in your bum,' she snarled.

Mr Big took a few deep breaths to calm down and think things through. This wasn't part of his escape plan. He lumbered back into the cabin, kicking Star out of the way. Mr Big sat in the pilot's seat and steadied the plane. 'Who cares,' he cursed, checking his watch. 'Your mum is probably dead anyway. "Spy Dog" they call her. I think we can now rename her "Dead Dog".' Mr Big laughed heartily until Star sank her teeth into his ankle. 'Get off me, mutt,' he yelled, kicking out at the puppy and sending her flying across the cabin again. 'You can keep the antidote,' he yelled. 'It'll be no use to you anyway. It doesn't work on dead dogs.'

Mr Big pressed the autopilot button and rose from his seat. He tugged at the bag leaning against the side of the plane and struggled to get it on to his back. 'Only one parachute,' he smiled. 'And it's mine.' Mr Big grinned as he pressed a button marked *FD*.

Ben was clutching the antidote tightly, ready to throw it to one of the puppies if Mr Big came at him. He didn't. The boy watched in open-mouthed horror as the criminal hauled open the aeroplane door. He checked the parachute was secure and waved to the passengers.

'I'm jumping for joy,' he yelled as he leapt from the aeroplane. 'Byeeeee,' they heard as his voice trailed in the wind.

Ben ran to the pilot's seat and looked

at the controls. 'What was that button he pressed?' he asked, frantically searching the dashboard.

'Here it is,' wagged Star. 'Says here that *FD* is *Fuel Dump.*' *Yikes!* thought the puppy, her tail drooping. *I don't much like the sound of that.*

A red warning light flashed on the dashboard and a female electronic voice announced very calmly, 'Emergency situation. Zero fuel. Please land the aircraft immediately.'

Ben looked at Star. Star looked at Ben. Spud wagged enthusiastically. 'At least we have the antidote,' he barked.

20

A FATAL MISTAKE

Lara lay in her basket. She was in a very deep sleep, her breathing getting shallower by the minute. The vet was just leaving, having given the stricken spy dog a thorough going over. He'd attached an oxygen mask to Lara in the hope of improving her chances.

'I'm awfully sorry, Mrs Cook,' he said. 'I've given her something to make her more comfortable but I can't cure her. It's a special kind of poison. We've run tests in the lab and we've never come across anything like it before. The professor was right—there is no known cure. I'm so sorry.'

'How long has she got?' asked Mrs Cook, wiping away a tear.

'Hard to say,' said the vet. 'But not very long. Maximum, an hour.'

Mrs Cook blinked more tears away and thanked the vet for his time.

'I guess this horrible man is the only

one who can save her,' sighed the vet. 'Now he's escaped, Lara is really out of options.'

Mrs Cook turned to Sophie and Ollie. 'Your brother's not come back yet,' she said, sniffling into a tissue. 'Where did you say he went again?'

Sophie tried to look innocent. 'Oh, you know, just for walkies with the pups,' she smiled.

'And the professor,' piped up her little brother. 'I'm sure they'll be fine.'

'The professor?' asked Mrs Cook. 'What's he got to do with it?'

'He wants to find the antidote,' chirped Ollie.

'Shush,' hissed Sophie, jabbing her brother in the ribs with her elbow.

'But it's a secret,' remembered Ollie, 'so I can't tell you any more.'

Mrs Cook took a deep breath and remained calm. 'What else *can't* you tell me, Ollie?' she asked in her special soothing voice.

'About them tracking down Mr Big,' smiled Ollie, powerless to resist.

Sophie smacked her forehead in frustration. 'It's Lara's only chance,

Mum,' she explained. 'The professor figured he was already in deep trouble so he may as well keep going.'

'And drag your brother into more danger,' yelled their mum, her cheeks reddening. She reached for her phone and punched in the scientist's number. She glared at Sophie as she waited. '*Professor!*' she screeched. 'Where are you and where is my son?'

Professor Cortex watched as Mr Big's plane disappeared into the distance with Ben and the puppies on board. 'Your son?' he asked. 'Benjamin?'

'Yes, Professor, my son Benjamin. Where is he? Is he safe?'

'Safe?' stammered the professor, his mind whirring. This was a double whammy. He hated lying. And he was terrified of Mrs Cook. 'He's taken the puppies up—I mean *out* for a spin,' he blurted, trying to avoid a blatant lie. 'Yes, a spin. Plane crazy they are. The three of them,' he added, as the dot of the aircraft shone in the sunshine.

'Are they with you?' asked Mrs Cook, calming down a little.

'Not *with* me as such,' admitted the professor, his brow perspiring and his brain racing. 'But I can see them,' he said enthusiastically.

'Well, you keep your eye on them until I get there, Professor. OK? Now where are you?'

'Will do, Mrs C,' he said. 'Don't worry, things are looking up,' he said, his hand over his brow as he peered into the sky.

21

A GLIMMER

Ben sat in the pilot's seat and surveyed the controls. 'So many buttons and dials,' he said, looking around frantically. Ben had flown a plane on his computer game but this was very different. 'Spud! Star!' he yelled. 'Get in here! What do you know about flying a plane?'

Star's tail wilted. 'Nothing at all, Ben,' she woofed. 'I've seen some movies but even spy pups can't land planes.'

'Especially not ones that have no fuel,' added Spud, tapping the fuel gauge.

The passengers fell silent as the left engine began to splutter. 'No way!' shouted Ben as the propeller slowed before stopping altogether. All eyes went right.

'At least that one's still work—' woofed Star as the right engine spluttered to a halt.

The three passengers desperately

looked around. There were a lot of emergency lights flashing on the dashboard. 'Emergency,' soothed the electronic voice. 'Zero fuel. Prepare for crash landing.'

Ben yelled in frustration. 'This is so unfair!' Wind billowed around the interior but the plane was eerily quiet. The nose began to turn downwards and Spud howled in frustration. 'We can't die. We have the antidote!'

Star left the cabin and jumped around in the back of the plane. 'Ben, where's your moby?' she woofed, putting her paw to her ear to demonstrate a phone. 'Maybe you can ring for help. Or send a Mayday message? Or we can phone Mum and tell her we love her. Anything!' she woofed.

Ben scrambled in the back looking for his backpack. 'Where's my bag?' he said, rummaging behind the seats.

'There,' woofed Star, pulling a backpack off a hook.

'No, that's not it,' he said. 'Mine's blue.' The nose of the aircraft was now tilting downwards and the three passengers held on. Ben came to the realization first. 'That's a parachute!' he yelled as he yanked it off the hook.

'So where's your bag?' asked Spud.

Ben shrugged. 'Mr Big must have put on my backpack, thinking it was a parachute. He jumped out of the plane with a bag containing some prawn cocktail crisps and a spare jumper!'

Prawn cocktail? thought Spud. *My fave!*

As they worked out what had happened, Ben's face lit up and the puppies' tails began to sway with excitement. All of a sudden there was a glimmer of hope. 'There's no time to lose!' shouted Ben above the noise of the wind.

The boy struggled into the parachute, tugging at the straps to make it as secure as possible. 'The plane's ditching!' he yelled. 'I'll jump and you two hold on to me. It's our only chance.'

'Yippee!' woofed Spud. 'I'm in. Come on, sis, let's do it.' Spud knew his sister was terrified of heights so he gripped her collar in his teeth and stuck his paws in Ben's belt strap.

Ben moved towards the aeroplane

door and looked out. The plane had already plunged through the wispy clouds. There was a patchwork of green fields below.

'Come on, Ben,' woofed Spud through gritted teeth. 'Do it!'

Ben held his breath and counted

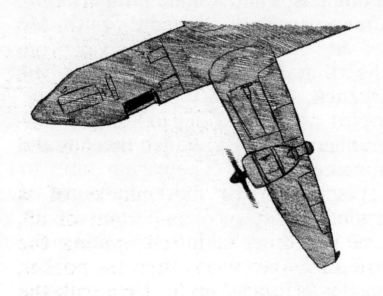

down from five. He closed his eyes as he leapt from the aircraft. He pulled the cord and the chute billowed above them, Spud nearly letting go as their sudden descent was abruptly slowed.

Ben and the puppies glided down from the sky, almost enjoying the experience. They landed with a *bump* and the parachute floated down on top of them. Ben tunnelled his way from beneath the material and undid the backpack.

Spud and Star bounced about with excitement. 'We did it. We actually did it!' woofed Star.

They stood in the middle of a cornfield. 'And, most important of all, we've got this,' said Ben, pulling the bottle of purple liquid from his pocket, 'and this.' He held up his wrist with the GPS watch strapped to it. 'This is officially the best gift from the professor. With the built-in satnav we'll be able to navigate home.' He glanced at his watch. 'Let's hope we're not too late!'

22

A SLOW GETAWAY

Spud put his powerful doggie nose to the ground and began sniffing. 'Rabbits,' he woofed. 'And chickens.'

'Our priority is to find transport,' said Ben.

Star's ears pricked as she picked up the sound of a tractor. 'This way,' she woofed, sprinting off across the field. The puppies chased through the corn, Ben in hot pursuit. This was a race against time.

They stopped to catch their breath at a farm gate. Three dogs ran to the fence and growled angrily. 'Stay off our land,' they warned.

'No need to be so horrible,' yapped Star. 'We need help. Our mum is ill and we have to get back home quickly.'

'Well, you can't come this way,' snarled one of the dogs. 'If you get in here, you might scare our sheep.'

Spud barked angrily. 'I think you're

more likely to scare them with your loud barking,' he replied. 'Listen, we need *urgent* help. Our mother is dying and we have to find transport to the nearest town. Being horrible to us is *not* an option.'

The dogs continued snarling at each other while Ben studied the satnav on his watch. He clicked the green button and a small arrow appeared. 'It's that way,' he shouted, pointing left. 'Ten miles. Home . . . and Lara. They're both that-a-way.'

All eyes went left. 'But it's just fields,' woofed Spud, gazing into the distance. 'With fences and hedges and cows!'

'So there's our solution,' woofed Star, jabbing a paw towards a nearby tractor in the farmyard. 'That's our best bet if we have to navigate through fields.'

Ben looked at the tractor, worked out what the puppies were suggesting and shook his head. 'I'm not so sure,' he said. 'I mean, how do you drive a tractor?'

'No idea,' yapped Star, sprinting towards the cab. 'But I'm a fast learner. We need action. And quick.'

The puppy bounded into the cab and woofed excitedly. 'The keys are in the ignition,' she barked, twisting her head and starting the engine.

Spud was halfway to the tractor when the farm dogs leapt over the fence to chase him. Three against one—and the one only a puppy! Star watched in horror as her brother was knocked off his feet. He rolled through the dusty farmyard and sat up, shocked. Before the dogs could attack he righted himself, hackles raised and gave his fiercest snarl.

Ben took his chance to leap into the cab and take the driver's seat. He ran his hands over the huge steering wheel. 'Easier than a plane,' he grinned. 'Hardly any buttons at all.' Ben's foot hit the accelerator and the tractor engine roared, black smoke blowing into the air. 'Come on, Spud,' he yelled, 'we've got a getaway vehicle!'

But Spud was blocked. The three horrible farm dogs crouched low, like hyenas stalking their prey.

Spud knew he'd never make it to the tractor. He remembered his karate lessons and jumped up on to his hind

legs. 'OK, dogs,' he said, 'if you insist.' Spud bounced around, shadow-boxing. 'Left. Right. Jab. Jab. Uppercut.' He snorted like a bull. 'Bring it on!'

The three dogs circled the puppy cautiously. His confidence was worrying them.

Spud was confident on the outside but a nervous wreck on the inside. *Three against one! Yikes! I need a spy-pup solution.* He knew he couldn't outrun them. *They're farm dogs: strong and fast.* He was fairly sure that the odds meant he couldn't out-fight them either. *My only chance is to out-think them.*

Ben revved the tractor and crunched it into gear. The farmer heard the rumpus and strode across the yard.

'What's going on here?' he yelled at Ben. 'What are you doing in my tractor?'

'Maximum confusion,' barked Spud, springing at one of the farm dogs and dodging through its legs.

The farmer jumped up on to the footplate of the tractor and rattled the door. 'What are you doing, boy?' he yelled. 'Unlock this door and get out of there!'

Spud took advantage of the confusion and scurried for the door of a nearby barn. He jumped at the latch. Everyone looked in horror as the door swung open and out poured the sheep. The three farm dogs panicked. Their sole purpose was to protect sheep and now the yard was full of bleating. The farmer jumped down from the tractor and ran across to help shoo the sheep back indoors. The attention was off Spud and he ran for the tractor. Ben lurched the vehicle forward and Spud jumped aboard.

'Which way's out?' woofed Star.

134

'Watch out for sheep!' she barked, covering her eyes as Ben wrestled with the steering wheel.

Ben checked his satnav watch and swung left. The farmer waved his hands in the air but it was clear that Ben wasn't going to stop. The man's hat fell off as he leapt out of the way. He shook his fist as the huge machine turned towards the metal gate. The gate was shut but there was no time to stop and open it, so Ben floored the accelerator. Black fumes belched out as the tractor demolished the gate and bounced into the cornfield.

Spud yapped with excitement as the tractor sped off, corn flying and rabbits running for their lives.

'A ditch,' warned Star as the tractor ploughed on. They hit the dip and Ben bounced off his seat and hit his head on the roof of the cab. Spud and Star held on for dear life as the tractor cut an emergency path through the field.

23

PLOUGHING ON

Sophie put a bowl of water next to her dying dog. Salty tears stained her T-shirt.

Lara opened an eye. *No thanks*, she sighed. *Too tired.*

Sophie put her fingers in the water and wiggled them around. 'Come on, Lara,' she coaxed. 'You have to drink. You have to stay strong.' She put her wet fingers near Lara's mouth and a pink tongue slurped.

Do you know what, thought Lara, fighting the urge to sleep. *I've had such a brilliant time. We've enjoyed some adventures. Thanks for sharing family life with me. I couldn't have chosen better.* Lara's mind was slow but her thoughts were clear. *Please take good care of my puppies.*

Then her eyes shut and she was back to sleep. Sophie patted her pet. There was almost no breathing now. 'Lara, I love you,' she sobbed. 'I hope the puppies are on their way.'

*   *   *

The professor hadn't known what to do. Mrs Cook was arriving at any moment and he was an intelligent man—he knew the difference between a spot of bother and deep trouble. He returned to his van and sat nervously. How on earth was he going to explain that Ben and the pups had taken off and were probably well on their way to Brazil with the most evil man on the planet? He wondered what came after 'deep trouble' on the scale of seriousness. *Even deeper? Deep doo-doos? Can you have infinity trouble?*

He flicked on his in-car computer. All the new GPS watches were working, so at least he could report on exactly how far they'd flown.

It felt like seconds before the Cooks' people carrier screeched to a halt and Ben's parents jumped out. They tapped on the van and the window slid down.

'Where are they, Professor?' demanded Mr Cook.

The scientist had a puzzled look on his face. He stared at the computer screen, than back at the Cooks. 'Honestly?' he said. 'Things aren't as bad as I thought. See these dots?' he asked, pointing to the screen. 'They've landed and are on the move.'

'Landed?' said Mrs Cook, her face turning pink with anger. 'If my Ben is in any danger—'

But Professor Cortex was too excited to worry about getting told off now. 'I promise I'll explain all of this,' he said quickly. 'But right now you both need to jump in. Let's go and get them!'

*   *   *

Ben was doing well. He'd navigated a field of cows and cleared two ditches. The tractor was muddied and battered but still going strong.

Star used her doggie watch to point out the directions. 'Five miles to go,' she yapped. 'That-a-way!'

The huge tyres meant that fields were no trouble at all, even muddy ones. Hedges could easily be breached

and streams crossed. The trio had found their way on to a country lane and were bouncing along as fast as the tractor would take them. Ben hit the brakes hard and the tractor stalled at a crossroads. He recognized the name of one of the towns. 'Not too far now!' he yelled, as he turned the key and the engine roared into life again.

The road widened as they approached the town. As they stopped at some traffic lights, they pulled up alongside Ben's head teacher, Mr Bell. There weren't many tractors in town. The man glanced up and the puppies waved.

'Hi there,' beamed Spud.

'We're just on a bit of an adventure,' waved his sister. 'We're spy pups, see. And this is a mission.'

Mr Bell looked at the puppies flapping their paws and then at the young driver. 'Benjamin Cook?' His brow furrowed and he removed his spectacles and gave them a clean. By the time he'd put them back on, the lights had changed and the tractor was gone. Mr Bell shook his head and decided he may need to go home and lie down.

Ben swung the tractor in the direction of Star's pointing paw. 'This way,' she yapped, jutting her leg to the right, 'across this car park.'

'Are you sure?' asked Ben. 'This is a supermarket.'

'Satnav says this is the quickest way,' woofed Star, nodding her head as Ben lurched the tractor through a hedge and down a bank into the huge car park. The mud-splattered tractor crunched through some empty trolleys. Shoppers leapt out of the way as Ben fought the steering wheel. Spud hid his eyes as Ben brushed a parked car and smashed into another before hitting the brakes.

'Whoops!'

Ben crunched the tractor into reverse and lurched backwards into a line of trolleys. 'Ouch!' Then forward into the car again. 'Sorry!'

Star helped him steer around the car park before they finally came to rest in a mother-and-toddler parking bay. The engine fell silent.

A crowd gathered as Ben gingerly stepped from the cab. The trolley attendant took centre stage. This was the most exciting thing that had happened in his twenty-five years as a supermarket employee. He took his notebook out and approached Ben.

'I'm sorry,' he said, 'but you can't park your tractor there. That is a family parking space.'

24

SUPERMARKET SWEEP

The professor's dashboard was beeping loudly as the van screeched into the supermarket car park and headed for the crowd. Mrs Cook held her hand to her mouth as she watched Ben get down from the tractor.

The trolley attendant was taking Ben's details as the professor leapt out of the van and interrupted. 'Aha,' he said, 'got you!' He grabbed Ben firmly by the arm. 'Please don't go near this boy. He's escaped from a . . . erm . . . secure institution. He's only twelve but is very dangerous. Look,' he added, pointing to Mr and Mrs Cook's stunned faces in the car. 'I've just captured the inmates who helped him to escape!'

'Yeah,' growled Ben, playing the professor's game. 'I'm Tractor Boy. Me and my dogs. We're going to plough up the world. Starting with this car park.'

The puppies bared their teeth and

the crowd stepped back. Spud snarled at a lady and she dropped her shopping. *Mmm, crisps*, he thought, snuffling through the carrier bag. *It's been so long since I had a full tum.*

Professor Cortex held Ben's arm behind his back like he'd seen police do in the movies. He manhandled him into the back of the van. 'In you go, evil Tractor Boy,' he shouted, overacting terribly. 'Your ploughing days are over. And your Tractor Puppies,' he added, before picking up the snarling dogs by their collars and throwing them in too. 'Good riddance to bad rubbish,' he said, rubbing his hands together. 'Citizens of the supermarket, you are now free to go about your business.'

The crowd cheered and the professor jumped back into his van. Mr and Mrs Cook sat inside, completely stunned. The curious onlookers parted to allow the professor through. He drove slowly between the pedestrians before slamming his foot down and screeching out of the supermarket car park.

'We've got it!' sang Ben from the back of the van.

'Got what?' snorted Spud, his head stuck in a crisp packet.

Ben held up a small bottle of precious purple liquid. 'This is the antidote that can save Lara.'

The professor switched on his siren. He'd never known such an emergency as this.

25

MR BIG'S MARVELLOUS MEDICINE

It was three days later that Lara woke. The puppies had been on twenty-four-hour watches for signs that their mum would recover. They'd taken it in turns and it was Spud's shift. Lara had taken the antidote but the professor wasn't sure they'd got there in time.

'An ordinary dog would have given up the fight for life by now,' he'd told the children. 'But GM451 is special. She's strong. If anyone can survive, she can.' But the professor had warned the family not to get their hopes up.

Spud's ears pricked as his mum licked her lips. Her eyes were closed but this was the first movement for three days. 'It's a good sign,' he wagged. An eye opened and Lara tried to smile a doggie smile.

'Hello, son,' she woofed.

Spud sped through the house barking

at the top of his voice. 'She's awake! Mum's awake!' he woofed as the family came rushing from all directions.

Sophie was first there, already snuggled up with Lara by the time the other children arrived. Ollie gave her a tummy tickle and Ben stroked her muzzle. Lara struggled to sit up and the puppies buried themselves in the warmth of their mum's fur.

'Lara, you're back,' cooed Sophie. 'We've been so worried!'

I've been a little stressed out myself, thought Lara, attempting her first wag in days.

'I bet you're hungry,' said Ben. 'Do you fancy something to eat?'

I'm starving, thought Lara. *But custard creams are off the menu.*

*   *   *

Lara sat at the table and wolfed her breakfast. 'So what's been happening?' she asked between slurps of her cornflakes. 'How did you get hold of the antidote?'

'We had to break Mr Big out of prison,' barked Spud. 'The professor came up with a plan and we got him out but he escaped.'

'Ben got to fly a plane,' woofed Star. 'And we did a parachute jump!'

Lara choked on her cornflakes. 'You did what?' she spluttered. 'Slow down and tell me in order.'

'Well, two jumps actually. The prof got in some major trouble because he helped break out Mr Big. Which was bad. And then let him get away.'

'Which was much worse,' continued her brother. 'But he didn't give up on you, Ma. None of us did. Professor Cortex figured he would have one last chance at getting the antidote.'

147

'And you and Ben ended up in a plane!' added Lara. 'I bet Mrs Cook wasn't very pleased.'

Spud looked around, a little scared. 'She blames the professor for everything,' he said in a hushed woof. 'The professor is in very hot water . . . scalding, in fact!'

Lara nodded. *He's been there several times before*, she thought. 'So what happened to the baddies?'

'Well,' began Spud, 'we used Archie and Gus as decoys while the main man escaped. They were easily captured. They didn't even get over the wall. We made sure of that,' he said, puffing out his chest with pride.

'And what happened to the main man?' asked Lara, sucking her banana milkshake through a straw. 'Mr Evil himself.'

'We wrestled the antidote off him,' wagged Star. 'And he jumped out of the plane,' she continued, her eyes huge with excitement. 'Except he had Ben's backpack on instead of a parachute.'

Lara spluttered bubbles into her milkshake. 'No way! No parachute?'

she said, wincing at the thought. 'So no more Mr Big.' Lara breathed a sigh of relief. She didn't wish harm on anyone but this evil man was bent on the destruction of her and her family. It was better that he wasn't around.

'So, with him out of the way, we can get on with living happily ever after,' wagged Spud.

'Can we please avoid any more adventures?' requested Lara. 'It's not good for my health!'

Star looked at Spud and winked. 'Course we can, Mum,' she yapped. *At least for a while.*

POSTSCRIPT

Mr Big's cheeks were flapping in the wind. He spread his arms and legs out like he'd seen parachutists do on the telly. 'This is brilliant!' he yelled to himself. 'I'm rid of the evil dog once and for all. And her blasted offspring. A fresh start for me. As soon as I land I can start building my criminal empire back up.'

Mr Big reached for the ripcord. He pulled the strap of Ben's backpack and a jumper floated by. Then some prawn-cocktail crisps made an appearance. *Not good*, he thought as he looked down. The ground was coming at him awfully fast. There was a lake down below and he twisted his body to aim for the water. As the ground hurtled towards him, Mr Big's life flashed through his mind.

It's been a good one, he decided. *Lots of lovely crimes. Some murders. They were ace. I even enjoyed my time in prison.*

Mr Big felt strangely calm as he headed for the water. He had time to calculate the odds. *I wonder if anyone has ever survived jumping from an aircraft and landing in a lake?*

There was a huge *splash* as Mr Big's body smashed into the water. The lake rippled and small waves lapped the shore. All was quiet as Mr Big's hairpiece floated to the surface.